MOTEL STORIES

WILLIAM TORPHY

Acknowledgments

I'm grateful to the many astute readers who have nurtured my writing with their feedback and support. They include Tom Jenks, Francesca Rosa, John Norton, David Jefferies, Sari Kossowsky, Cynthia Kreuz-Uhr, Richard Schwarzenberger, Saand Choden, Joe Meltzer and Marc Jampole. A special thanks to Ken Weingart, whose photographs partly inspired *Motel Stories*. Many thanks to James Mitchell at Ithuriel's Spear and deep gratitude to the people at Unsolicited Press.

Earlier versions of these stories appeared in the following literary magazines & journals:

A Sweet Kid," *Bryant Literary Journal*, Spring, 2020
"Birds of the Lesser Islands," *Miracle Monocle*, 2018
"Hideaway Lounge," Pendust Radio audiocast, 2020
"Royal Flush," *ImageOutWrite*, 2016
"The Good Son," *Bryant Literary Journal*, 2019

This collection is dedicated to my parents, who encouraged me to pursue my own creative path, and whose concern for the marginalized and commitment to social justice continue to inspire me.

TABLE OF CONTENTS

MOTEL STORIES

WILLIAM TORPHY

BIRDS OF THE LESSER ISLANDS

First of all, you should know that I'm not attempting to arouse sympathy, which can sometimes be an unhelpful and insipid thing. These are simply the words of a much younger woman, a younger me, a girl tossed into unfamiliar circumstances, but who was fortunate enough to escape serious damage. It's a story that I have told in part but never fully until now.

During summer back home, birds from the Northern Hemisphere fly thousands of miles south to escape the cold. They nest in the flame trees and banyans and perch on the beaches of our tiny island. Whenever I took my little brother, Gumabay, to watch them, I would clap my hands as he stared in wonder at what seemed to be white flowers rising from the trees' branches to form feathered clouds in the sky.

My name is Bagaoisan, which in Tagalog means to sprout wings. My *ina*, my mother, named me. I sometimes think she possessed the gift of prophecy.

I've been in America for six months. I search for these birds on my walks around my new home. Harry tells me that I must not wander through other people's lawns, but I ignore him. I don't care if his neighbors think I look foolish shivering in the morning fog in my white bathrobe wrapped tightly around me.

A gray cat with black stripes and white paws follows me. His shiny coat and full body tell me that someone takes good care of him. I play a game, the same one I played with Gumabay. I stop in my tracks suddenly, and turn to face him. The cat halts and stares up at me. I pick up my pace, and he pads swiftly behind, his footprints in the wet grass trailing my own. I've named him Mockingbird.

Harry is a big man who likes bland food. I could not believe my eyes the first time he took me to a supermarket. So much to eat, packaged in so many different ways. But no smells attracted my nose, no vendors shouted from their stands, and no shoppers haggled over prices.

"Where are the fish? The chickens and the pigs?" I asked.

He sighed and led me to a long, cold coffin at the back of Crystal Farms. I laughed when I saw the bloodless meat covered with plastic.

"You need to get used to how things are done here," he scolded, as he tossed a few slippery packages into the shopping cart.

Back home, my family raised chickens and grew almost everything we ate. When I first arrived here, I naively imagined the Crystal Farms family must have worked very hard to offer so much variety of food. I soon discovered that it's a giant company with thousands of workers who are mostly immigrants, like myself.

My father, my *tatay,* was a gambler. He visited the *jueteng* stall every week and was always in debt. Whenever I had asked my ina why she put up with it, she would just shrug. "It is one more cross I need to bear." When I asked her just how many more crosses she needed to bear, she peered at me with an aggrieved expression. "You ask too many questions."

I attended the island school for longer than my older

brother and sister, but still, like them, I was put to work at an early age. I helped my mother to mend the fishing lines and sell produce from our garden at the market. She always hid a bit of the money she made in a safe place where my father couldn't find it.

One day, as I was tending our garden, my father called to me from his hammock. He went straight to the point. "I've made a very fine arrangement for you. You will marry a rich American named Harry." He was grinning, as if he was proud of this accomplishment, but his eyes looked shrewd.

"I did not ask for this arrangement," I told him.

His smile disappeared. "You will do as I say. I am your father."

When I threatened to throw myself into the sea, he picked up a switch and shouted, "Would you ruin your chance for a better life?" He was the one looking for a better life. I was not the first girl on the island whose father had collected dollars for an arranged marriage.

"I will run away, "I told my mother. "He will have to return the money the American paid him."

She looked at me with alarm. "And where will you go? Your brother and sister will never defy their father and take you in. You will be without a home, with no family to protect you."

Homeless, and bringing disgrace to my father. It seemed that I had no choice in the matter. But even though this might be true, I had long before decided that I would never let anyone cause me hopelessness, no matter where my life might take me.

Harry and I live in a town called El Sobrante, which means "the leftovers" in Spanish. It also means "the end of the world," according to Harry's mother. Unlike my island, which is flat and barely above sea level, it is hilly here. People keep to themselves. They drive their cars into garages and disappear inside their homes.

My village was filled with noise. Pots clattering on iron stoves, animals screeching and grunting, children laughing and playing games, parents shouting, and neighbors squabbling.

The only sounds here come from the distant freeway, and from the Spanish-speaking men who mow the grass, trim bushes, and blow leaves from one area to another.

They joke among themselves, but whenever I wave and greet them, they appear anxious and pretend to be busy. I think Harry has warned them not to talk with me. He seems to have no friends, and knows people only from his work. There is also his mother, of course, who refuses to admit that I exist.

Everyone in the village had gathered to wish me goodbye. Ina hugged me tightly. My father wore a new barong shirt and shiny new shoes. His wager, with me as a bride, had paid off. Gumabay wrapped his thin arms around my legs and cried, "I don't want you to go!"

I peered down at him and tousled his unruly hair, trying to hide my own tears. "I will see you again. You'll be a big boy, then."

He clutched me tighter. "I don't want to be a big boy when I see you next time."

I kissed him on the forehead and slipped away, knowing I might never see him again.

I waved to everyone from the fishing boat that carried me from our island to a bigger island, where I boarded a ferry. Three American men were smoking on the deck. I wanted to ask them about California, where the man my father called

Harry lived, but the words would not come.

An old man resting on a bench noticed my interest. He said they were returning to Manila from a hunting trip. "They come every year to shoot migratory birds on some lesser island. They do it only for sport." he whispered, as if admiring men who enjoyed the luxury of shooting only for fun.

I prayed they would never visit my island.

It took more than two days to reach Manila. When the ferry docked, the passengers crowded the ramp and scattered in all directions, like birds fleeing a predator. I was greeted by an impatient-looking man wearing a confident expression.

"The American, Harry, hired me to escort you to the airport," he said, shoving papers in my face and pushing me into a taxi.

As we crossed a bridge, I could see buildings even taller than banyans. They rose above fields filled with shacks, yards cluttered with laundry. The taxi moved slowly through crowded streets clogged with thousands of honking cars and brightly painted buses. People rushed in all directions. It was shocking to realize how immense and bustling humanity was, feeding off the earth like flies on a fruit pie.

A young boy stared out from the open window of a passing van, reminding me of Gumabay. I saw a man strike a woman across the face at a street corner, and prayed that I would not be treated badly in America.

I flinched when my escort placed a paper on my lap. "You need to study it. This is what Customs will ask you when you arrive in the United States."

It was a list of questions and answers written in Tagalog. I gazed at the first answers. "I'm currently a citizen of the Philippines… I have nothing to declare…"

"Why are you coming to the United States?" my guide

asked sternly.

"I am here to meet a man named Harry."

"No!" he corrected. "You must say, 'I'm meeting my fiancé to get married.' It's very important that you remember this. Customs will look for inconsistencies. They will try to trick you."

The lines at the airport seemed to stretch for miles. My escort pointed to a sign.

"San Francisco. That one is your flight." Once we approached the front, he shook my hand, wished me a safe trip, and disappeared into the crowd.

We had barely spoken, but I felt that my last connection with home had vanished.

The man in line ahead of me was being searched by security. If I refused to be searched, I wondered, would they send me back home? No, then I would have to face my father's anger. He might carry out my empty threat, and drag me by my hair and throw me into the sea.

I often imagined myself as a bird in flight. The reality of flying in an airplane was a different matter, and I was very nervous when I boarded. A Filipino woman stood, smiling as she let me pass to my seat at the window. When the plane jerked to motion and bounced down the runway, I cried out. The woman took my hand.

Her voice was calm and steady. "What is your name?"

"I'm Bagaoisan."

"I'm Tala Torres. Is this your first time in the United States?"

I nodded, and said that I was marrying an American.

Her smile disappeared. "Do you have family in the States?"

I shook my head.

"So, you're all alone then?" Her expression turned serious.

Her eyes seemed to bore into me, and I turned away to gaze out at the billowing clouds. I was more than just alone. I felt empty of myself. My past was disappearing as we soared higher than any palm swift bird.

"...arriving in San Francisco in thirty minutes."

I opened my eyes, vaguely remembering the dream I'd had. Gumabay drifting out to sea, palm swift birds circling his body.

The lights of a city appeared below as if by magic. Fog was creeping past a bridge and scattering into the land. A small prickle of excitement pushed through me as I stared down at it all. But, then, a terrible fear gripped me, and I began sobbing.

The woman—Tala—grasped my hand again and squeezed it lightly.

Once our plane landed, people rushed from their seats, eager to escape their confinement and to join their families and friends. But I was in no particular hurry to meet a stranger.

Tala Torres walked with me until we had to separate. "It was very good to meet you, Bagaoisan. Please call me if you ever want to talk." She reached into her purse and handed me a card. *Women's Defense Network.* Her name was printed under it.

She embraced me, and I held on to her, longer than I had my mother.

I didn't understand what the man at Customs was saying. Another agent appeared and took me to an empty room. A young Filipino woman came in and asked me several questions in Tagalog. I had memorized all the answers perfectly, and so I was released.

A crowd waited at the end of a long hallway. A balding man stood off to the side holding a sign with my name on it. The lights reflected against his glasses, and so I could not see his eyes.

I put on a smile. "Are you Harry?"

He stared at me with a look of surprise, as if he hadn't been expecting me.

My throat felt like the sandpaper my father used to smooth his boat. "I am Bagaoisan." I pronounced my name slowly for him. "Ba-go-wee-san."

His hands were shaking, crushing a bouquet of white flowers against the sign. He mumbled, "How was your flight?"

I told him that I had met a nice woman on the plane, but didn't confess how frightened I had been at first.

Harry silently led me to baggage claim. He frowned at my battered suitcase, but took my arm gently as we walked to his car.

I stared out at the city, with its hills dotted with lights. We crossed a long bridge to the other side of a bay. Yet another crossing leading me farther from home.

The moon cast a shadowy light on the hills surrounding Harry's house. I wanted to walk and smell the air of this place, but he drove directly into a garage and then led me through a door into a bright kitchen that looked as if it had never have been used. I thought of our squat, makeshift stove back home, the dented pots, and the recycled jars where we stored our rice and mung beans to protect against insects and rodents.

"This will be your realm," he declared, as if that too was all pre-arranged. I glanced around the sparkling room with its appliances, all lined up like a queen's court waiting for attention from their ruler, someone from a distant land who had reluctantly inherited the crown.

Harry took me through the house. The big rooms, with tall windows looking out into the night, somehow seemed empty of life. He directed me into his den. A television screen covered an entire wall. He pointed to the opposite wall and proudly pointed to framed honors he had received from a university, and the awards he had collected from the company he worked for.

I followed him upstairs into a bedroom. He asked me to sit on a bed he called a California king. I had trouble imagining this oversized, plain-looking man as the king of California.

He kissed me and fondled my breasts like an awkward man milking a goat. I told him I was sorry, but that I needed to sleep. I was still flying high above the Pacific Ocean, and had barely slept since leaving home. The next morning, Harry pulled back the covers and gazed at me like one of his awards before he left to take a shower.

He joined me later in the kitchen, dressed as he had been the night before, in a plain white shirt and black pants. He pulled a box from the cupboard, filled two bowls, and handed me a spoon. The rainbow-colored cereal tasted like sugary sponges. Lucky Charms. It was strange to be served by a man, though I realized that I would soon be expected to serve him.

The telephone rang, and he asked me to answer it.

"Is Harry there?" It was the voice of an older woman. "It's his mother."

"Hello. This is Bagaoisan. I'm looking forward to meeting you."

"Please get him to the phone."

Harry shook his head and whispered, "Tell her that I've left for work." He was asking me to lie, just as my father had whenever the bill collectors came around.

His mother hung up without leaving a message.

Harry handed me a note. It was written in Tagalog: *I will come today and give you instructions on your duties. Maricel*

I wondered how many people Harry paid to bring and to keep me here.

When he left for work, Harry told me not to leave the

house. Instead, I stared out the windows at a cloudless sky. The brown hills dotted with trees seem to stretch on forever. I was like a bird that had migrated to an unfamiliar world.

I woke up to noise from the kitchen. A woman with tight curls and a stern expression stood at the counter. "You must be Bagaoisan. I'm Maricel. I brought some food for Harry and a few things from the Manila Market for you."

She reached into a bag to take out delicacies that I thought I might never taste again. I grabbed the calabasa squash and stroked the dark green skin covering its golden flesh. I inhaled the inviting scent of coconut wafting from the fresh bibingka.

"Thank you. I will make *ginataang* calabasa and cook shrimp in chilies with coconut milk for Harry."

Maricel shot me a sharp look. "These are for you only. Harry has an American stomach and doesn't like spicy food." She emptied a second bag filled with cans of soup and packages of frozen dinners. "These will have to do until you learn to cook like Harry's mother."

"You have much to learn." She settled a pair of glasses on her nose and led me through the house, pointing out all the features and conveniences. "This is how to do the laundry. First, you press this button for the time. Then press here for the cycle. And this button is for…

She must have noticed my confusion. "You'll get used to it, and then you'll wonder how you ever lived without it."

The vacuum was simpler. In the den, she cautioned me about damaging Harry's framed awards, and then demonstrated the remote. "We have a Filipino channel, but don't waste too much time watching it. You'll improve your English faster if you watch the other channels."

She took me back into the laundry room. I had loaded the washer incorrectly. Impatience etched her forehead as I held a pair of Harry's undershorts dripping on the floor.

I had so many questions to ask her. Where her family was from, how long she had been in the United States, what her life was like here.

"We may have time to talk about those things someday. But you are no longer living on your lazy little island. You're in America now, where there are always things to do."

Harry returned from work late. I had made a stew that Maricel said was his favorite, adding a few peppers, but he told me that he had already eaten. I gorged myself on bibingka while he watched TV in the den.

Later, he called from the bedroom. His body was pale, like a ghost's. His eyes grew bright when he asked me to undress. I pretended that I was a heron on a beach, the waves washing over me. It was over quickly, like a phantom's appearance. As soon as he started to snore, I stood under the shower and wept for the first time since leaving home.

The next morning, watching Harry leave, I turned to go back inside and discovered that I had locked the front door behind me. I ran into the street and waved, but his car had already disappeared at the bottom of the hill. I checked the door again. It didn't budge, and there was no one around to help me.

A cat appeared at my feet, purring and rubbing his sides against my legs, arching his back to meet my hand. I stroked the fur on his back, gray with black stripes, and touched the patch of white that dotted his nose and matched his paws.

The situation was hopeless and so I decided to take a walk. I passed houses painted the same light brown color as the hills.

The cat trailed behind me, so I decided to call him Mockingbird. I discovered a small park at one end of our street. Mockingbird settled next to me under a tree. To relieve my anxiety, I told him about the island where I was born, about my village and my little brother, Gumabay. I described the long journey I had just taken. All the while, he nuzzled his nose against my hands, commanding me to pet him. It was his price for listening.

The sun had disappeared behind the hills and fog was tumbling over them like ocean waves. I traipsed back to Harry's front door, with the cat following. It had suddenly turned dark. Only the security lights from the neighbor's houses marked my way. Mockingbird rubbed against my leg and then darted away to disappear under a fence, leaving me alone on the porch.

Harry returned much later, shouting from the car, "What the hell is this?"

I explained that I had accidentally locked the door.

"You've been outside all day?" He grabbed me by the arm, pulled me inside, and led me upstairs before ordering me to take a hot shower. I glanced at my reflection in the mirror. The person I saw, with her wild hair and red-rimmed eyes, resembled a *multo*, a spirit who appears after death.

Harry was waiting for me, naked on the bed. The California king, a white mountain. I once again imagined myself as a heron, this time skimming the sky, freed from the earth.

Later, I escaped downstairs. Searching through the kitchen drawers, I discovered a brochure picturing Filipino women in provocative poses. "Lusty Asian Ladies." Was that what Harry expected me to be? Is this what my father had promised him?

Maricel returned the next day with more bags of food and

old magazines from back home. "Read these only when Harry is away," she warned. "He expects you to focus only on him when he's here."

I thanked her for the magazines, but told her I preferred walking to the market myself.

"Everything is too far away. Harry might sometimes take you in his car. But he won't have much time for that. He's married to his work."

"Does that mean he cannot marry me?" For one brief moment, I was a bird in flight again.

"No," she laughed. "That's just an expression."

She watched me as I put away the food. "One more thing. Your name. It's too difficult for people here to pronounce. Let's shorten it to Bago."

Bago. It sounded so ugly. Two syllables, alone, without the other two to complete them. It was like being cut in half.

Harry's mother came to visit that night. He introduced me proudly, like one of his awards. She ignored me all during dinner, frowning and barely touching the chicken I had prepared Harry's way. I knew what she was thinking. My son has made a big mistake bringing this nothing island girl here to marry.

I would not let her manipulate me. Like myself, she would just have to make the best of it, at least for the time being.

After his mother left, Harry kissed me sweetly. But I knew that it was a lie, a prelude to laying on top of me. He was not a cruel man, but he was wrong to think that I was assigned to him like some project at work.

"You'll be eighteen in two months," said Maricel. She opened the computer to show pictures of wedding dresses. "I think you'll love this pale yellow one. It's the same color as jasmine, our national flower."

I told her that I preferred the blue one. Yellow or blue, it didn't matter. I hated them all, a satin cage.

Later, we sat in the den, eating lumpias and watching the Filipino channel. A woman appeared on the morning show. It was Tala Torres. I remembered her kindness, and the knowing look she gave me as we parted, as if we were destined to meet again.

I leaped from the sofa. "I know her! She sat next to me on the plane."

Maricel clicked off the television. "We don't need to watch this."

I grabbed the remote and turned it back on. Tala Torres was describing how women around the world were being sold as servants and sex slaves.

I threw the remote down. "Is that what I am? A slave?"

She looked offended, or at least pretended to be. "Harry is not a criminal. He's a good man. You are lucky to be here."

"Is it lucky to be taken away from your family without having any choice?"

"You should be happy. You'll be married soon."

"Married to a giant boy who eats sugary Lucky Charms, but tries to control me as my father did!"

"Listen to me, Bagaoisan. I came here the same way you did. The only difference is that I was brought here by a Filipino man. I've made the best of things. I have children, just as you will someday."

"Neither of us had a choice."

I didn't tell her that I had kept Tala Torres' card in the dresser drawer, hidden under my clothes.

This morning, I learned that a terrible typhoon has battered my country. The sea has washed away many small islands. Villages have been scattered like driftwood, and thousands have drowned.

I called Maricel, who told me that her family in Manila was safe, and promised to find out news about my island. I left the house. Mockingbird was waiting for me on the front porch. I confessed to him how frightened I was for my family, but he grew distracted by sparrows nesting in a nearby tree. Everything seemed prey to attack.

Tonight, I had a terrible nightmare. Gumabay stood alone on our beach. He called to me as a giant claw emerged from the water, closing around him and carrying him out to sea. I woke up tasting my tears, and I must have cried out. Harry stared at me as if I were a bulbul bird perched in a tree. The expression on his face reminded me of those hunters on the ferry. I challenged him silently with my eyes before he turned away with his back to me, and quickly fell asleep.

It came to me then, a memory so clear that I nearly doubled over. Gumabay on the shore, waiting for me to clap my hands and scatter white flowers from the banyans' branches. I pictured all the birds, homeless from the storm, circling their lost chicks floating in the sea.

I imagined myself sprouting wings then and flying back home. But there was no returning. I had stepped into a new life, a life I was resolved to form on my own terms.

THE GOOD SON

I couldn't face everyone's questions, their judgments. Even Shirley at the bank gave me an incriminating look this morning when she handed me my canceled savings book along with the $457.45 from my account.

I'm on a Trailways bus now, staring through foggy windows at mounds of snow piled on the side of the road. We've stopped in practically every town since I boarded. Aurora is so far north that my sister, Kat, jokes that it might as well be in Canada. The dictionary definition of *aurora* is dawn, but for me it means dull. Forests surround it. Dawn arrives late, and darkness comes early, especially at this time of year. I've basically lived in the wilderness with grouchy bears all my life, but I'm out of the woods now, traveling on the Interstate through open farmland. Silver silos and farmhouses. Frozen ponds and beaver dams. Battered cornstalks stretching to the horizon.

San Francisco. That's my plan. To stand on top of one of its hills and scatter small town restrictions to the wind. I've wanted to leave home since I can remember, but I never imagined it would happen like this. I know people in town are talking about me, shocked that such a good son could turn out to be such a big disappointment. They'll focus on the sex part, not that I was a coward and lied to save my own skin.

I imagine Mom is crying a Jordan River right now, and Dad is royally pissed. They'll go to church on Sunday, and the entire congregation will pray for my "safe return." Like I've been kidnapped or abducted by aliens. Pastor Larry will read the parable of the prodigal son, but everyone will be thinking of Leviticus.

Kids at school called me a fag. I thought it was because I was a brown-nose honors student. I memorized *Webster's Unabridged* backward and forward and won the county spelling bee two years in a row. I was even going to compete next year in the 1987 State Championship. Not exactly the qualities that make someone Mr. Popular at my high school. Once in a while, a girl would tell me that she'd kill to have my thick brown hair and long eyelashes. But I was almost as skinny as I was in junior high and had a case of acne that my doctor called "moderate," but looked like the Pyrenees Mountain range to me.

I tried out for the track team because I ran fast. That was how I dated girls, too. Running. Always double-dating because it was safer. Fewer opportunities to make-out, more opportunities to make excuses.

Matt Hendricks never hid the fact that he liked guys, which took a lot of courage in a town like ours. He tried to start a Gay-Straight Alliance group at school last year, but our principal Mrs. Greggs claimed it was "inappropriate for a Christian community." Except for Matt's friends in theater, no one would have joined anyway.

Gym class had always been purgatory for me, but it must have been hell for Matt. Coach Willits warned the boys to "guard your asses with a pansy in the showers."

The jocks harassed him. "Matt's a fag! Matt sucks dick. Matt's a pussy!"

He must have worked out all last summer. When Matt returned to school this Fall, he was—shock and awe—all muscles. Even his braces were gone. He was an A+, a hunk like the centerfold models in the *Playgirl* magazine I once shoplifted at Jacobson's Thrift. He parodied the jocks, strutting around the halls in tight T-shirts with an ironic swagger. Girls started flirting and prayed for his conversion. a good-looking guy whose daddy owned the biggest supermarket in town.

I pretended I was only taking an objective, scientific interest in his metamorphosis (*Webster's Unabridged*), but I developed some pretty wild fantasies. Matt and me making out in the men's shower room after school. Matt and me jerking off in the choir loft at church. Matt and me doing it in the produce section of his daddy's store. I even started to shadow him. Stopping near his locker between classes. Standing next to him in chemistry lab. Sitting at the table where he ate lunch with his clique of theater girlfriends.

Mystery meatloaf was on the school lunch menu yesterday. I decided I'd grab a Hot Pockets at home, and headed toward the shortcut along the river.

I spotted Matt's car near the bridge in the corner of the parking lot. Bronski Beat's "Smalltown Boy" was playing on the radio. I pretended to ignore him. He rolled down the window and shouted, "Hey, Robert. It's cold outside. How about a ride?"

My groin said yes, but I shook my head just the same.

His smile was as wide open as his passenger door. "I have the new Whitney Houston CD."

Who was he trying to fool? First of all, Whitney was fag city. Second, I knew his used Escort didn't have a CD player, which had just come out for cars. But before I realized that I'd even made a choice, I was there sitting next to him.

Matt chattered on, something about the homecoming dance decorations, but I didn't hear a word. I couldn't take my eyes off his full lips, his breath cloudy from the cold as he talked.

I swear I don't remember making that first move. I kissed

him, and tasted his tongue. He kissed me back, and pulled me against him. It was like falling into a deep well with no bottom. As his hands began working their way inside my fly, I automatically pulled away. But then I didn't want to. He tugged down my pants and grabbed my junk. I closed my eyes and dropped my head back against the headrest. It took, like, maybe twenty seconds and then it was over.

The windows had turned foggy from us making out. When I opened my eyes, I saw two hazy faces pressed against the glass. It was those snitches, Emily and Sarah, who started making gobbling sounds like turkeys on speed.

"Dick suckers! Ass packers!"

The Scandal Sisters' jeers attracted a gang of guys smoking behind our school. Smelling blood, they surrounded the car and began pounding on the hood, whooping and shouting through the windows.

I pushed Matt away, yanked up my pants, and stumbled from the car. "He offered me a ride. But it was just an excuse to put the make on me!"

My lie must have been what set them off. They pulled Matt from the driver's seat and shoved him around. "Cocksucker! Faggot!"

Matt shouted back, "White trash hicks!"

They tossed him on the ground and started kicking, snarling and howling like a pack of hunting dogs on a deer. Matt curled into a ball and wrapped his arms around his head to protect it. The lips that I had just kissed were bleeding. I could taste the blood, like clenching a metal knife between my teeth.

Coach Willits' blew his whistle. Mrs. Greggs rushed toward us with a troop of kids following her. I ran off, my pulse beating in my throat. Halfway home, I heaved my breakfast onto the frozen riverbank. Luckily, Mom and Dad were both at work. I grabbed a juice box from the fridge and stumbled upstairs to my bedroom, slamming the door and collapsing onto my bed.

I knew the news would spread like a grease fire. Mrs. Greggs would report "the troubling incident" to her assistant, and people would soon be repeating the gossip to shoppers at Mr. Hendricks' Foodway. By the end of the afternoon, some busybody at work will be asking Mom if she has heard. And Mom, after getting an earful, will tell Dad.

And Dad… I buried my head in a pillow. I was dead meat.

Hail pounds on the roof of the bus and beads the windows in crystal tears. The landscape outside looks like it's underwater, all distorted like a Salvador Dali painting. We're passing a Native American casino with a neon wigwam glowing on the roof. It reminds me of the so-called "genuine Indian powwow" our folks dragged Kat and me to watch one summer. There are loads of monster trucks and SUVs in the parking lot. Inside, white folks are emptying their wallets at slot machines and gaming tables. The Car Castle Auto-Clean next door is closed up. My dad always says, "What's the sense of washing your car in the middle of winter, anyway?"

Mount Pleasant. One mile. I don't see any mountain, just a Texaco station and an Arby's. Everywhere, signs on the road. *Free Alignments.* I definitely could use one of those right now. *His & Her Hair Salon.* Which option should I take?

The bus pulls to a stop outside Carson's Family Restaurant. *Closed for the Winter.* A family huddles together at the curb. They look like they might be from Mexico. Someplace south of the border, anyway. The father hugs the boy and girl to protect them from the biting wind. He's wearing a straw hat that truck farm workers wear in the summer. The mother blinks against the snowflakes swirling in the wind. She's not much taller than her kids.

The pneumatic door opens with a hiss, and a blast of freezing air whips through the bus. The family gathers their belongings, and the mother climbs aboard. The boy and little girl follow, with the father behind. The boy pokes his sister in the stomach and giggles. His father says something sharp to him in Spanish. *"Portate bien!"* I remember that phrase from my one year of Spanish, and from seventeen years of living in a strict household. Behave yourself.

I opened my bedroom window and lit a joint Kat had given me for "personal emergencies." The smoke curled around my anxiety, and I started to float far from Aurora, until the front door slammed. Afraid that it might be Mom, I extinguished the joint on a sandal. Boots dropped on the mat with a thud and someone began tramping up the stairs, sounding like a herd of horses. It could only have been my sister.

Kat is two years younger than me, but she was always way more advanced in certain departments. She's confident and outspoken, and totally rebellious. She skipped school with her friend, Annie, and talked back to our parents. She even defied their curfews.

Dad sometimes got so angry that I thought he might hit her. He even once threatened to send her away to Christian boarding school.

"I think I must be adopted," Kat once told me. "Maybe I was a crack baby."

Kat called me Mr. Suck-Up. She teased that I always played it safe. I was the Good Son, and she was the Bad Seed. Still, we confided in one another. She told me that she was having sex with Brad Daley. When I confessed that I had "a thing" for Matt Hendricks, she didn't seem at all surprised.

"I know you better than you know yourself, Rob."

Yesterday, when I heard her coming upstairs, I thought she was going to bust my balls about what happened during lunch break Instead, she made a beeline to the bathroom. I could hear her barfing. She flushed the toilet and then knocked on my door.

In our family, our bedroom doors were supposed to remain open unless privacy was absolutely required. It was probably some guideline our parents read about in *Midwest Christian Family*. Kat usually barged into mine, anyway, always hoping that she'd catch me doing something embarrassing.

She knocked again. "Robert, can we talk?" She sounded pleading, and when I opened the door, her eyes were red, like she had been crying. She plunked down on the bed next to me and resurrected the joint from my sandal.

"Guess what. You're famous. The entire school is blathering about you and Matt Hendricks making out in his car."

Busting my balls, for sure. "That's not true. He came onto me and I tried to fight him off."

"Give me a break. Like, didn't you tell me that you had the hots for him? But why did you have to do it in the school parking lot, for God's sake.

"It was really terrible, Kat. Those guys beat the crap out of Matt."

"I know. I was eating lunch with Annie when the ambulance came. They took Matt to the ER."

My fantasy boyfriend. In the hospital, thanks to me.

"I'm totally screwed. There's no way I can go back to school. And Dad and Mom are going to kill me."

Kat screwed up her face and looked like she was going to cry. I was surprised that she was so upset about it.

"Mom and Dad are going to kill us both," she said. "It's gay conversion-therapy camp for you this summer and permanent exile for me." My sister, usually so defiant, had a sad, crumpled look.

"What do you mean, exile?"

"I'm pregnant."

I thought she was joking. "I *have* noticed that you've gained weight lately. And your hair looks kind of dry, too." I reached out to check for split ends, but she swatted me away.

"I'm with fucking child, dammit." She drew her knees up to her chest and hugged them. "Annie knows a doctor and I'm making Brad pay for it."

"You're getting rid of it? You can't do that, Kat!"

"Oh, for God's sake, Pastor Larry. Just think. Brad, a daddy? Like that's ever going to happen."

She lay her head against my shoulder. I put my arms around her and told her that everything would be okay, that at least she had done it with a member of the opposite sex. But I secretly wondered if her "little problem" might divert Mom and Dad's attention from my own.

The Mexican family stow their bundles in the overhead and claim two rows of seats, the kids in front of the parents, across the aisle from me. The father takes the mother's hand and kisses it, reminding me of how lonely I am. The boy wrestles off his coat. He's wearing a red stripped sweater underneath. He pulls out an old RadioShack console from his backpack, like my very first one. His sister stands a doll on her lap and makes it do a jerky dance.

I had a doll once too. I wanted a Ken but settled for an ugly troll I found at a yard sale. I teased its bright yellow hair and made clothes for it from the scraps I found in Mom's sewing room. The troll was homely and weird, and so it was easy to pretend it wasn't a girl's doll. I felt ashamed, but excited about playing with something forbidden. *Only girls play with dolls.* That's how I felt when I stepped into Matt's car.

The bus driver's voice blares over the PA. "Dubuque! Fifteen minutes." The sides of the road are jammed with fast-food restaurants, strip malls, and subdivisions covered with heavy snow. The sun suddenly appears from behind the clouds, like a fanfare, illuminating a Wal-Mart before it retreats back again.

The kids across from me look bored. They're both staring at me with big brown eyes, as if I offered some kind of entertainment. It must be tough traveling on buses all the time. I hope we stop long enough to grab something to eat.

After Kat left for Annie's, I called the Gay Crisis Line. I had called once before and talked with a guy named Mark, who had a nice mellow voice. He told me that he hadn't come out until college, and that I had something to look forward to.

A guy named Stewart answered this time. "We're here to help. Tell me why you've called." He sounded like he was reading from a script. A little geeky, too, like someone who was volunteering because he couldn't find a date.

I told him what happened with Matt. He asked me if I was in any physical danger. I told him that Matt got beat up, but I was at home and wasn't planning to go to go back to school.

"Being outed publicly isn't easy, Robert. Have you talked with your parents about being gay?"

"No way. They would totally freak out. They believe gays go to hell."

"Is there anyone you feel comfortable talking with? A counselor, or maybe a minister?"

Was he kidding? Pastor Larry always managed to insert something homophobic into his sermons every Sunday. Our high school's guidance counselor was a retired Marine sergeant who thought "gay recruitment" was a communist plot to undermine the US armed forces. My homeroom teacher attended the same church as my family.

Before I could reply, I heard the front door open and paper bags rustling.

"Sorry, Stewart, but I have to go."

"We should finish our discussion." He sounded petulant as if he were being jilted. I hung up.

Mom was calling from the bottom of the stairs. "Robert?"

A few minutes later she was at my door. I opened it, yawning, pretending that I had been asleep. Her forehead was wrinkled with worry. Her hair, usually lacquered in tight curls, hung loosely around her face.

"Emily's mother stopped by work this afternoon."

Of course, she did. A busybody and a cunt, just like her daughter.

"She mentioned something…disturbing…about you and that boy, Matt. You were seen in his car, and, well, Emily's mother said there was an incident. You've never given your dad and I any reason to think…"

"Matt asked me to help him with a trig problem, but he was using it as an excuse to make a pass at me. I ran from the car and—"

"I pray that your father hasn't heard anything yet." She gave me a plaintive glance as if the news was too much for her. "We can talk about this later. I should put the groceries away now."

Mom avoided confrontations. She also needed to believe that I had done nothing wrong. I was a good son, after all.

I stayed in my room until Dad called me down for dinner. I told him that I wasn't hungry. It was a house rule that we pray together before our meal. I was tense at the table, especially since Kat wasn't around to deflect things. I pushed the peas and potatoes around my plate, trying to make them disappear, and asked to be excused early. I thought Dad must not have heard anything yet, since he seemed to be normally consumed with eating his dinner.

Kat called me later from Annie's house. "Matt is still in the hospital, but at least he's not in a coma or anything. I thought you should know."

I breathed a sigh of relief. "What about the jocks who beat him up?"

"Two of them were taken to the station, but they were released. You need to tell the police what happened."

"Are you kidding." There was no way I was going to file a report.

"It's all going to come out one way or another."

"You mean, like you and the baby?"

"That's real nice, Robert!"

"I'm sorry, Kat." My mind had started working fast. Going back to school wasn't a viable option. My reputation in Aurora was wiped forever, and I was yet to face the wrath of Dad.

"I think I might be leaving, Kat. I can't take this town anymore."

"Leave? You can't be serious. I'll be all alone then."

"You have loads of friends here."

"But I won't have my brother."

"You'll still have me. I won't be around for a while, that's all. You'll be okay. You're much stronger than me."

"I'm not as strong as you think. Please don't leave."

"I can't keep lying anymore. And telling the truth is never an option here."

"Then go, you traitor!" She hung up.

I should have called her back, but what else was there to say?

After my parents went off to bed, I stuffed some clothes into my backpack, along with my dictionary.

This morning, I pretended that I was going to school like always. Instead, I nursed a hot chocolate at Ella's Cafe waiting for the bank to open. Tula, the oldest waitress in all creation, eyed me suspiciously.

"Aren't you supposed to be in class?" she asked, pulling up her support stockings.

"I have a dispensation for the day."

She shook her head. "You use all those big words. I should keep a dictionary behind the counter."

After I emptied my savings account, I stuffed the wad of money into my pocket, and felt something loose at the bottom. It was the silver cross and chain my parents gave me as a gift for winning the spelling bee. I marched down Pine Street, and then sprinted like a track star, racing to catch my bus.

An old guy in the station's restroom smiles at me. I ignore him. The café is closed, but the vending machines are working. I grab a soda and a Snickers, and head back to the bus. The wind pummels my face. My lungs are tight. This bus *is* supposed to be heading south, right?

Two men are arguing with the driver. They're wearing camouflage jackets and orange hunting caps and holding rifle cases. They look like kissing cousins of that survivalist guy back home who lumbers into town every few months to stock up on cigarettes, jerky, and beer.

"You're not allowed to take those rifles onboard," the driver insists. "Interstate Transportation Rules. They need to go in the baggage compartment."

The older guy's face turns red. "We stowed them overhead on the other bus."

"I don't know about the other bus, but you can't bring them on mine."

The younger guy shifts his cap backward, grips his rifle case, and takes a couple steps toward the driver.

"Easy, Eric," his friend cautions. "We need to get to Des Moines by nightfall."

His words sound like some dumb cliché from an old Western movie.

The driver checks his watch. "You boys need to make a quick decision. My bus is leaving in two minutes."

"This is total bullshit!" shouts junior, red-faced, scraggly hair sticking out from under his cap.

I haven't exactly had an easy time with angry straight men lately. I retreat to the bus and take my seat just in time to see the Northwoods grizzlies stash their cases in the compartment below.

Angry Eric stomps aboard, shouting, "Motherfucker!" He shoots murderous looks at everyone on board before claiming an aisle seat, colonizing it with a farting thud.

The Mexican kids are sitting behind him playing a game of patty-cake and sing-songing in Spanish.

Junior turns, scowls at the kids and shouts at no one in

particular. "What the hell are wetbacks doing on our bus, anyway?"

That's real nice. I'm sure he'd find a defining word for me too. Fag, fairy, cocksucker. Pansy, poof, queen. Cock jockey, donut muncher, fudge packer. Ass bandit, bone smuggler, or maybe butt pirate. I've heard them all. How did Matt take it?

The kids' father peers at the hunter as if he's a piece of broken farm machinery.

"Who are you staring at, spic?" His friend from across the aisle suppresses a chuckle.

The muscles on the father's face twitch. I get the feeling he could handle both of these guys at once if he had to. His wife places a hand on his thigh as if to restrain him. He tells his boy and girl to move to the row behind them.

Meanwhile, the xenophobe stands and stretches, revealing his hairy beer belly. "You should all be goddamned deported! You hear me, Jose?"

The family just stares at him.

"What's wrong. No parlo Americano?" He tramps back to the toilet and leaves the door open, cursing each time the bus hits a bump. He emerges while zipping his fly and pats the little girl on the head as he passes by.

The father stands, offense furrowing his face.

"Sit back down, wetback."

It's like a switch has suddenly flipped inside of me. I bolt up from my seat. "Why don't you leave them alone."

A hostile sneer appears on the hunter's face. "What you going do about it, faggot?"

"You're a cacophonous cretin with a puny phallus."

His friend is choking with laughter. This only makes his pal angrier. He lurches toward me, his fist clenched.

"Cut this out right now!" shouts the driver from the front.

The bus edges off the highway and lurches onto the shoulder. The driver scrambles from his seat and strides down the aisle to face the hunters.

"Shut it down, if you guys expect to stay on this bus. I have the right to throw you off for good cause. You can claim your rifles in Des Moines."

Junior growls, "We aren't doing nothing,"

The driver waggles his two-way radio in the air. "Or I can contact the highway patrol. Your choice."

The older hunter raises both hands in truce. "Cool it, Eric. I want to get home without any more trouble."

His pal puffs, flicking his fingers at the driver in some kind of surrender.

I realize that my fists have been clenched all this time. My palms are etched and red with pressure from my nails.

The father nods at me while touching his heart, and whispers to his wife. She reaches into a bundle on the floor, pulls out a package wrapped in waxed paper and hands it to me. "Un burrito para ti," she declares. "You enjoy."

Her smile nearly makes me burst into tears. I've felt mostly numb for the last two days. Leaving home has left a void inside of me.

I reach into my pocket, take out the silver crucifix and chain, and place it in the woman's hand. I even manage to cobble together a sentence in Spanish. *Quiero que lo tengas.* I want you to have it.

She peers at my gift with surprise and attempts to hand it back. I shake my head. She finally closes her fingers around it. "*Muchas gracias, señor.*"

It's the first time anyone has called me sir.

"Des Moines in twenty minutes!" shouts the driver. "And none too soon, either."

He pulls a frown in the rearview mirror. The hunters slouch in their seats, silent.

I dream of wolves, snarling. A wounded deer, and tracks of blood across the snow. Mexican kids are dancing at a fiesta along with their parents. Kat is holding up a squalling newborn baby for me to inspect.

I wake up wondering if I had dreamed it all. Matt's lips against mine. Boys so frightened of what might be inside themselves that they could kill. Kat telling me that she's pregnant. Deciding to leave home.

The moving landscape outside reminds me that I'm on a bus. We must be in Nebraska now, and I glance across the aisle. The family has vanished during the night at some stop along the way.

A sheet of paper ripples on the seat next to me. It's a kid's drawing. A boy asleep on a bus. He's shown in profile. A row of lollipop trees appears outside his window. Bright yellow rays from the sun stream across a blue sky filled with puffy white clouds. There's even a rainbow that stretches across the horizon.

Another boy stands by the side of the road. He's dressed in a red-striped shirt, waving with a hand so big that it looks like a baseball mitt.

MOTEL STORIES

THE MAN WHO DANCES WITH DOLLS

A thrill of anticipation rose as Larry Reitman drove into the heart of Hollywood with his silent beauties. Shirley sat in the passenger seat while Betty rode in the back. Rose and Tiffany lay next to his suitcase in the trunk.

Larry possessed the pale, unhealthy-looking complexion of someone who never ventured into sunlight, no small feat in Southern California. Balding, middle-aged, and pudgy, he had a social life that was limited to lunches with people from work. His wife had divorced him long ago after learning that his regular weekend "business trips" were actually liaisons with a woman named Shirley.

He took the Hollywood Boulevard exit. His eyes brightened when he spotted the neon sign blinking against the oily murk of the LA night sky. Two of its letters had burned out ages ago. The ones that remained dimly announced the motel's questionable status. UNSET IN. The Sunset Inn had seen better days, certainly, but it served his needs. and he maintained a standing weekly reservation for Room 8.

He turned into the driveway and parked his Buick directly in front of his room. Locking the car, he headed to the office. The manager's silhouette was a dark blob against the blue light of an ancient TV, tinfoil twisted around its rabbit ears.

The manager gave him a knowing look. "Good to see you again, Mr. Reitman. Room 8 is ready for you, as usual."

Reitman took the key, saluted, and quickly left.

He's an odd son of a bitch, thought the manager, but not the Sunset's strangest customer, not by a long shot. The man had been coming to the motel for five or maybe six years now, more predictable than the van that restocked the vending machines or the city's truck that picked up the trash.

When Reitman checked in for the first time, the manager's curiosity had been aroused as he watched his guest unload a peculiar cargo. Later that night, he peered through a gap in the room's curtains. What he had seen was certainly bizarre, but no more so than what went on in other rooms on a Saturday night.

Larry entered his room and switched on the two bedside table lamps. They cast a harsh glare, illuminating spiderweb cracks on the walls and ceiling, highlighting puzzling spots in the green shag carpet.

After a quick inspection, he returned to the car and took Shirley into his arms. Carrying her inside, he lowered her gently onto the closest of the two queen beds. He returned to bring Betty in from the back seat. He propped the pair up against the bed's headboard, arranging them with their legs exactly parallel and faces turned toward one another. Shirley and Betty were like sisters, sharing secrets and momentous tales of seduction.

Always about him, of course.

He lifted Rose from the trunk, followed by Tiffany, and toted them both inside. After draping the two over the small table, he made one last trip to collect his suitcase along with a paper bag packed with bologna sandwiches and Gatorade. He glanced across the parking court and into the office where he could see the manager pouring himself a drink.

Back inside, Larry rubbed his hands together, exclaiming, "We're all going to have another special weekend, ladies!"

He pulled an air pump from the suitcase. A shrill hiss broke the room's silence. Within seconds, Rose and Tiffany began to expand into life.

He removed two frilly numbers from the case, and dressed Betty in a filmy pink chemise, Evie in a pale green negligee. After they were fully inflated, he dressed Rose in a transparent black teddy that complemented her shapely body, and chose a red lace bikini set for Tiffany. Tiff was the youngest of his girls. She was his wild card, a playful tease who pretended to resist his advances. He sat her in the tattered lounge chair and splayed her legs over its arms.

Steadfast Shirley sat on the bed attentively. She was his first. With her short curly hair and no-nonsense nightgown, she exuded an aura of mature confidence. She had exceeded her warranty long ago, yet she hadn't aged a day since the night they first met at Adam's Adult Emporium.

Larry draped red scarves over the two lampshades to create a romantic ambience, and surveyed his seraglio with satisfaction. "Ladies, you look gorgeous, as always!"

He undressed to a sleeveless undershirt and boxer shorts before peeling off black compression socks from his calves. He never felt embarrassed with his girls. They never made fun of him. He was the only man in the world as far as they were concerned.

He swallowed the blue pill with a sip of Gatorade, and excused himself to shower. The bathroom smelled of mildew and Pine-Sol, but the water was always hot. He sighed in the billowing steam, shedding the boredom of his week working for the accounting firm. After he dried off, he peered into the foggy mirror and saw himself transformed into a much younger man. His skin was imbued with a healthy glow, his hair darker and somehow fuller. He felt a faint stir in his groin.

Wearing a spotless white T-shirt and boxers printed with red hearts, he stood before his lovely ladies with confidence now. Shuffling through a pile of CDs, he inserted his favorite into the player. The mellow voice of Dean Martin filled the room, crooning, "You're Nobody 'Til Somebody Loves You."

Betty gazed at him with admiration. Rose and Tiffany waited for his attention. He drew Shirley into his arms, and they began to dance.

THE THING ABOUT SCOTCH

Edward's hands were shaking like castanets. He tossed the razor into the sink and stared at his reflection in the hazy, pitted mirror, grimacing at the bleeding gash on his chin. His face, once passably handsome, had fallen into soft furrows, his eyes underscored by dark circles. He resembled the motel itself: aging poorly, etched by transient sadness, and devoid of any luster it had once possessed.

The thing about Scotch was that it helped him zone out, but it could also throw him into deep brooding. Last night, he had felt captive to a repetitive film, an endless tape loop of personal slipups and fuckups. A "damp, drizzly November of the soul." A line he had read in *Moby Dick* a long time ago.

Seven o'clock. The housekeepers would arrive soon. Guest check-out at noon.

He grabbed a push broom and headed for the driveway. Hollywood Boulevard was quiet on Sunday mornings, empty of traffic. The tourists, junkies, and working girls were all still asleep. The sidewalk was a toxic dumping ground, scattered debris from Saturday night's debaucheries. The tinsel town glitter of broken glass, fast-food wrappers, takeout cartons, condoms, cigarette butts, roaches, beer cans, and syringes. He swept a pair of soiled aqua panties into the curb.

Yesterday, Homeless Jimmy had dragged a trash bag into the entrance and kept kicking at it, mumbling unintelligible nonsense and screaming obscenities. As Edward rushed from the office to chase him away, the man jumped on the bag, strewing garbage across the driveway.

Attempts by the city to improve this part of Hollywood Boulevard had failed. The bright new trash containers were trashed overnight. The saplings that he had faithfully watered in front of the motel were quickly reduced to twigs. The city had commissioned artists to paint murals on the shops' pull-down doors, but their work could only be seen after the stores had closed. Gigantic, graffiti-scrawled likenesses of Bogie, Crawford, and Madonna peered at disoriented tourists and the horde of zombie souls who inhabited the street at night.

He squinted into the slanting morning sunlight at an empty pink party bus lumbering past a disheveled Elvis impersonator singing "Love Me Tender" as he pissed against a wall. He loaded the collection of debris into the bag and dragged it to the motel's service room.

Maria had already parked her utility cart in front of an early checkout's room.

Luisa, her eyes red and puffy, stuffed her purse into a locker. "Good morning, sir."

"*Buenos días, Luisa. Cómo estás?* " He always made a point of greeting the housekeepers in Spanish.

Rogelio, wet hair combed back from his forehead, was shouting outside Room 1. Its open door revealed a churn of men inside, yawning and pulling on clothes for work. They were all undocumented, and paid the ex-Mexican cop a nightly fee to sleep on the floor. Edward had admonished him for abusing these men, but he wasn't prepared to give up the deal they had made to split the proceeds. It was a transaction he kept off the motel's books.

Retreating into the office, he shook Rice Krispies into a bowl and sniffed the milk carton. His years in these quarters with its rattling mini fridge, thrift store TV, and single bed didn't match the life he had once envisioned for himself. Not that his ambitions had ever been anything but modest. A bungalow with a backyard, and a wife who could tolerate him. He had been attractive to women once, with a full head of dark hair and confidence to spare, but his veneer of indulgent charm had worn off as fast as greyhounds ran at the track.

Margaret had stuck with him for a time, but she eventually wised-up and left, taking the dog and the car keys. Except for the divorce papers, she had communicated with him only once, writing to tell him that she had a daughter—his daughter—and had married a man in Michigan soon after Alice was born. He had wanted to ask about the girl, but there was no return address. He often wondered if he would have given up drinking and gambling if he had been allowed to raise her.

He could barely recall all the jobs he had run through—bartender, bookie's assistant, knockoff luggage vendor, phone solicitor. He was always paid under the table, the unreported income a perfect setup for social insecurity. He seemed to have run out of options the day he spotted the Manager Wanted sign posted outside the motel. The owner had managed the Sunset Inn himself for decades and was ready to retire. Edward had come to the motel from everywhere and nowhere, the perfect qualification for a job tending to travelers. He was hired.

Sixteen years later, and he was still here.

He pushed the cereal bowl aside and peered out the office windows. Sunshine had invaded the parking court. A shirtless guest lounged outside his room, smoking a cigarette. Luisa was handing over the extra towels that Reitman in Room 8 always requested for his "girls." He sometimes envied the crackpot, a character who fully lived in his own fantasy world.

To assuage his own loneliness, he had once taken in young

men from the street, assigning them work around the property in exchange for food and a place to sleep. He treated them as if they were his sons. They usually turned out to be trouble, peddling drugs to motel guests or stealing petty cash from the till. Not that he was exactly a saint in that department himself.

There was only one kid that he regretted losing. Terry was just off the bus from Missouri, the Show Me State, and claimed to be eighteen. He was honest and a good worker, but cocksure like most kids his age. He baited Rogelio and made fun of his machismo. One day Terry called the man out for harassing the housekeepers, and Rogelio tore into him. Edward nursed the boy's wounds until he took off one day and never returned.

He sometimes wondered why he hadn't left by now himself. But where would he go? He was shackled to the motel, like a prisoner with no one waiting for him outside the gates. And now even this dismal prospect seemed uncertain. The owner's son, a Bel Air attorney angling for his inheritance, was trying to convince his father that the Sunset Inn was no longer a profitable asset. The land, however, could be sold for a fortune.

Edward swallowed the dregs from his coffee cup and poured himself a finger of Scotch. He flicked on the radio. Patsy Cline crooned "Sweet Dreams (Of You)." The lyrics, nostalgic and regretful, made him think of Alice, the daughter he had never gotten to know.

SKY BLUE

A baby blue Jaguar, like a piece of the sky, pulled to a stop in front of the motel's office. It was a sublime thing to behold, like James Bond's car from the Roger Moore era. A man in his early forties sporting a stylish haircut stepped out from the passenger side. His clothes looked expensive, but there was a certain carelessness in his appearance. Sport coat creased, silk shirt rumpled, and light brown loafers scuffed as if he had just come from an all-nighter.

The driver remained in her seat. Edward could see her legs through the open passenger door, long and shapely against the tan leather interior.

Her companion stumbled into the office and slammed the door against the wall.

"Watch it!" barked Edward. "We can't get replacements for that louvered glass anymore."

"Why would you even want to try?" the man mumbled, standing unsteadily at the counter.

Edward laid odds that he was high on something. Most likely coke, all hyped up like that. He could smell alcohol on the intruder's breath, like a toxic cloud.

The man drew a finger up to his mouth. "You want to know a s-secret?" he hissed. "In the strictest confidence. I'm with a very sexy lady, so I'm asking for your finest room. The VIP suite, if it's still available."

He snickered, amused by his joke at the motel's expense.

"You've come to the wrong place. This isn't the Chateau Marmont," replied Edward evenly.

The man tapped an impatient fandango on the counter with his fingers. "I'll take whatever you got, then, as long as it's clean."

"That'll be eighty dollars." Room 2 and 7 were unoccupied. Like most gamblers, Edward held the number seven in particular esteem. He'd hold that room for someone who wasn't such a pretentious wiseass.

The man jammed his hand into his pants pocket, only to come up empty. "Shit! I must've lost my wallet. Back in jus' a minute." He slammed the door again, and careened toward the Jaguar.

"Baby, I'm really sorry," he whined. "I must've left my wallet someplace."

"You always do this to me," the driver complained. She opened her purse and shoved a wad of bills into his hands.

The man slipped a few twenties into his jacket pocket before he dropped the remainder on the counter. Edward counted them out, debating whether or not to keep the extras. The accountant would be none the wiser. He decided against it and returned the balance.

"Is there someplace where I can get decent bourbon?" asked the man.

"The minimarket next door will have something on the top shelf. But first, you need to sign in."

The man scribbled a name, Stephen, into the register and then scurried outside. He handed his companion the room key along with a plastic baggie before disappearing into the street.

The woman stepped out of the baby blue. Edward came around to the window to get a better view. Her silvery dress shimmered in the light, making her movements appear almost kaleidoscopic. She was middle-aged, but definitely a looker. Her face was framed by a mass of auburn hair. He noticed that her eyes were unnaturally bright. The eyes of a cokehead. And her expression, mouth turned down at the corners and cheeks that drooped slightly, seemed to possess a weary disappointment, the cast of someone who had allowed life to slip through her beautiful hands.

Edward was sure he'd seen her somewhere before.

After the usual parade of pay-by-the-hour afternoon guests, Edward heated a frozen dinner in the microwave and poured himself a drink, before settling in front of the TV. He preferred the old shows, reruns from the '70s and '80s. His favorite was a series that followed a filthy rich oil family from Texas. In tonight's episode, the patriarch summons his daughter and berates her for wanting to marry a young man who he suspects is a gold-digger. The father threatens to disinherit her, but she remains stubborn and defiant. The camera comes in for a close-up on her face as she shouts, "Nothing you can say or do will stop me from marrying the man I love!"

"That's where I've seen her before!" shouted Edward. He had read something about that actress in a celebrity tabloid left by a guest. Susan Douglas was one of those flash in the pans whose sole claim to fame was her role as the beautiful but rebellious daughter in *Houston*. The tabloid recounted her fraught personal relationships and detailed her problems with drugs and alcohol, her unsuccessful treatment at several clinics.

He poured two fingers of Scotch into his glass. "What the hell is she doing here?" He was saddened by his discovery but comforted by the knowledge that he had never risen so high only to fall so low.

Edward promised himself that if he survived the upcoming audit, he would stop filching from the till. He would even cut down on the drinking and gambling.

Susan lay on the bed, staring at the rash of mold that seemed to be creeping toward her from the bathroom door. She had come down fast. Stephen said he was going somewhere to score for them again, but she knew he wouldn't return.

She switched on the TV and clicked apathetically through a stream of shopping channels, religious programs, and sport shows, until she paused on a brutally familiar scene.

A young woman's beautiful face is distorted with resentment and rage as she screams abuse at her controlling father. Eyes ablaze, she turns away and stomps out of his wood-paneled office. In the next scene, hell-bent on self-destruction, she is seen speeding in her sportscar through a barren landscape of dry scrub brush and oil derricks.

Susan watched, captivated, until she couldn't look anymore. She switched off the TV and buried her head in a pillow. That had been her first important role, the one that had defined her in the popular imagination. As vain and headstrong as that rich, young girl, she had chosen to follow the same pattern in her real life.

More than anything else, she wished the script she had written for herself could be torn up and thrown away. She would demand a retake, edit the miscues, erase all those bad decisions that had destroyed everything promising, that had led her to this desolate room.

Stephen was lost somewhere. Another party, no doubt. She would pretend that she had never been here. She washed her face and applied lipstick before walking over to the office. She dropped the key on the counter with finality, startling the manager from his torpor at his desk.

The sun settled on the horizon like a broken promise, as her Jaguar sped toward the Pacific. She wanted to feel the water lapping at her bare toes, to lose herself in its glimmering surface. She might surrender, at last, to the ocean's undercurrents, roiling with unexpected consequences, and washing over her.

LEAVINGS

Luisa loved her two children with all her being, but it was hard raising them alone.

She left the apartment at six a.m. five days a week to catch the bus to work. Her neighbor, Dorothy Gonzales, whose children were grown and out of the house, prepared breakfast for Alfredo and Juanita before seeing them off to school.

She dreamed of the day she could quit her job cleaning up other people's leavings. She often imagined herself relaxing at a spa as she changed the soiled sheets, replaced the thin towels and brittle bars of soap, scoured the sinks and toilets.

On her first day working here, Edward, the motel's manager, claimed she would be collecting "good tips" from the guests. But she seldom received any, other than the coins left on night tables or lost under chair cushions. The customers at El Toreador, where she waited on tables, weren't rich, but they were generous and supported their own.

She loaded her cart with supplies from the service room and pushed it outside. Groggy men dressed in rumpled T-shirts and jeans filed out of Room 1 and headed out toward street corners and parking lots in search of work.

Rogelio collected money from these day laborers, and warned her to stay away from them. "Never enter the Pit. Those braceros are horny bastards." He grinned suggestively. "You could get yourself into trouble."

He was the one she needed to avoid. His hands were roving

nomads.

One day she heard Rogelio shouting at one of the workers, accusing him of stealing. She watched helplessly as he slammed a fist into the poor man's jaw that sent him to the ground. Minutes later, another man, compact and muscular with silver flecks in his dark hair, emerged from the room. He bent over Rogelio's victim and held a cloth to the gash on his chin before helping him to his feet and handing him a few bills.

Maria, the motel's other housekeeper, confided that the good Samaritan's name was Hector. She had spoken with him once at the café next door. He was a day laborer like the others, but he acted like a caballero, she said, a gentleman.

Luisa kept her eye out for him, even venturing into the café before work one morning. He was not there, but they nearly collided as he was leaving the motel. He nodded at her and smiled before they both hurried on their way.

Several days later, she was surprised to find Hector standing outside the service room. He told her that he noticed how hard she worked, and wished her *Buenos días* before he left for the street. He appeared again the next morning with his hair combed and wearing a collared white shirt. He asked if he could buy her something to eat after work. She agreed to meet him at the café. They ordered coffee and pastries. To hide her discomfort, she showed him photos of Alfredo and Juanita.

"They're beautiful!" he exclaimed. *"Y el padre?"*

"There is no father at home."

He studied her face for several moments, and then confessed, "I have no children, no wife." He told her about his village near Oaxaca. "I could not provide for my wife," he admitted. "When I came to El Norte to find work, I wasn't always able to send her money. She ran off with another man."

She knew all about these leavings. In her case, it was the

man who had disappeared.

Hector walked her to the bus stop and asked if he could see her again.

"I work at the motel five days a week. I'm sure you will see me there."

He smiled at her coy reply. "I would like to see you away from the motel."

She nodded without comment, and he kissed her, just a peck on the cheek. She touched his chest and felt the fullness of his muscles under his white shirt. It had been such a long time. Her bus pulled to the curb, and just before the door hissed open, she asked if he would like to come to her place in Echo Park.

"I will take you and your kids somewhere nice," he promised.

On Sunday, Hector arrived with little toys for Alfredo and Juanita, and flowers for her. She had prepared pozole and *mole de pollo* for lunch. Afterward, they took the bus downtown to Grand Park, where they fed tortillas to the ducks and enjoyed ice cream. Little Juanita held Hector's hand. Alfredo looked proud walking alongside a man. Luisa could tell that he was good, someone she might be able to trust.

"He's not one for you," Maria cautioned. "He's undocumented and has no future."

Already thinking about a future with Hector, she didn't answer.

She met him at the café whenever their work permitted. One day, he walked her all the way home, and stayed for the night. The next morning, as he drank coffee at the kitchen table, Alfredo and Juanita sat close to him and told him they didn't want him to leave. They all took a bus to Venice Beach together that weekend. Hector once again stayed the night.

Luisa grew worried when he didn't appear at the motel for three days. She worked up her courage to ask Rogelio if he knew where he might be.

He stood so close that she could feel the heat of him. "I know you two are *amantes*," he declared, moving even closer.

She pushed him away. "I'm only asking if you have seen Hector."

He smiled darkly. "There was a raid at his work site. ICE detained three of the men and La Migra took them away. Hector was one of them."

A dense, black fog released itself inside her, but she tried to hide her emotions.

"Do you know where they took him?"

He shrugged. "Where they take all the illegals. They send them back home." His eyes gleamed. "But if you ever need anything from me—"

"No, *gracias*," she mumbled, rushing toward the service room. Hector was gone, swept up like the debris she cleared from the motel rooms.

Maria discovered her bent over a pile of used towels. "Edward is asking for you. Those gringo pigs in Room 5 want to stay for another night, and he needs you to—"

Luisa stared up at her, sobbing.

"What's wrong?"

She placed her head against Maria's shoulder and tried to explain what had happened to Hector.

"I'm very sorry. I know you liked him."

Embarrassed, she nodded, and tried to dry her tears.

"I'll cover for you," offered Maria. "Finish your work when you are ready."

Luisa collected herself. She knew what was required no matter the circumstances.

Work hard for the sake of her children.

She straightened her blouse and left the service room. Rogelio was waiting for her. She glared at him. His expression shifted suddenly, from arrogance to uncertainty.

"Well, *señora*, you always know where to find me."

She gripped her cart tightly, and pushed it along the asphalt over discarded cigarette butts and abandoned gum that she would clean up later. Those gringos, always leaving their messes for her to pick up.

Rogelio stalked away, muttering, "Damn that woman. She's a hard one."

Inside the Pit, he found two exhausted workers curled up on their mattresses. He glanced around the room, searching for Hector's duffel. He found it under a blanket and rummaged through its contents. He pulled out a worn photo and held it up to the light. An old man and woman, likely Hector's parents, stared apprehensively at the camera as if they harbored premonitions of their son's fate.

Rogelio dug deeper, under a denim shirt and a tattered pair of jeans. He pulled out a pair of black dress shoes in which a brightly colored tie and a shiny new belt were coiled.

"Where did that stupid *cabrón* think he would use these?" he growled.

As his fingers reached the bottom, he felt something lumpy and pulled it out. Slipping it into his pants' pocket, he crept past the two men snoring like out-of-tune trumpets in a mariachi band.

Back at his apartment, he opened the envelope and spread the cash out on the kitchen table, counting. One thousand, two thousand. Two-thousand-four-hundred dollars in all! He imagined what he would do with that cash. Forget Edward's lousy lotteries and sports-betting schemes. He'd buy himself that flat-screen TV he'd been wanting. Maybe take a weekend trip to Vegas. Get another tattoo added to the masterpiece on his back and find himself a good-looking *mujer* to entertain him.

He stuffed the bills back into the envelope, opened the freezer, and hid it under the frozen dinners, where he stashed all his cash. He had seen someone do that in a movie once, though this precaution was probably unnecessary. Who would dare break into a badass, ex-cop's place? They would be paying a visit to the cemetery if they tried.

Rogelio approached her as she tossed wet towels into the hamper. Luisa grabbed a handful of clean linens and hurried into the room. He leaned against the open doorway.

"I have something for you, Luisa."

She told him to go away and slammed the door, listening from inside until she heard his footsteps recede across the asphalt. Placing the mop into its slot on the cart, she spotted an envelope sitting on top of the hamper, with her name scrawled across it.

She opened it and read the note inside: *Hector asked me to give this to you. — Rogelio.*

She stared at the thick wad of bills. Retreating into the room and slumping on the bed, she counted. Twelve hundred dollars! More money than she had ever seen at one time. She didn't understand. Wasn't Rogelio the kind of man who would ignore Hector's request and keep the money for himself?

He would certainly expect something from her now. She was tempted to throw it back in his face.

Instead, she crossed herself, kissed the envelope, and pushed it into the pocket of her apron. Tomorrow, Sunday, was her day off. She would take Alfredo and Juanita to Mass in the morning, and they would pray for Hector's safety. She would also pray for protection against the endless hunger of men.

PAMPERS

The cabdriver pulled away from the curb so fast that Maggie barely had time to grab her bag from the back seat. What the fuck was his problem? She was a good fare, picked up at the group home in Echo Park for a straight shot down Sunset and up Western to Hollywood.

As she entered the motel's office, her baby wailed, flailing her arms and legs. The man behind the counter scowled at her like she was a kidnapper. "I'd like a room for one night."

"Room four is available. Checkout time is eleven a.m.," said the manager.

She shifted the baby to one side and reached into her purse, pulling out the cash she had saved. He counted out the bills before he turned over the room key. Edward, his name tag said. He was a drinker like her father. She could tell.

"My brother is visiting me here later. He may come into the office asking for me. Would you let him know my room number?"

"Why don't you just call him?"

"I don't have a phone." She wasn't about to ask this crank to use the office phone, and finding a public phone within fifty miles was zero.

The manager scrutinized her. "Your brother, you say? Who should he ask for?"

It never stopped—people being suspicious of her—like she had a mark on her forehead. She poked a finger at the register.

"Just like I wrote right here! Maggie Hilmer."

"And what's *his* name? What does he look like?"

This asshole asks more questions than her counselors. She just wanted to get to her room, feed the baby, and crash. "Brian. His name's Brian. And last I knew, he's medium height with sandy brown hair that's cut short. He wears black-rimmed glasses and dresses very nice. What's with the interrogation?"

The manager raised his hands in mock defeat. "It's just a precaution, in case some nutcase on the street saw you come in, steals a look at the register and asks for you. I try to protect my guests, especially young women."

She huffed and grabbed the key for Room 4. Hiking the baby to her shoulder, she stormed out of the office. A muscular, tough-looking Latino guy stood across the parking lot, acting like he owned the place. He gave her a quick appraisal. Forget creeps on the street. This place crawled with them.

Maybe it hadn't been a good idea to ask Brian to meet her here, after all. But she needed some time away from those Nazis at the halfway house, even if it was just for overnight. Brian asked her to come to his apartment in West Hollywood, but she didn't want to listen to any crap from his boyfriend. She had once overheard Carl tell her brother, "I can't believe that Maggie and you actually came from the same family."

After she became pregnant, Brian had offered to help. She took the money but told him that she had more help than she needed from the counselors and the nurses. The clinic had taken her up as some kind of pet project after she confessed that she wasn't cut out to be a mother. "Now, dear, let's not throw the baby out with the bathwater," her social worker admonished. As if.

She sometimes wondered if she had kept the baby just to spite them all. She'd had only one relapse during the whole time, and the baby was just fine. Her tiny fingers and toes intact. Her bright brown eyes and thatch of dark hair, legacies from her father.

She hung the Do Not Disturb sign on the doorknob and turned the bolt lock. The baby howled, flailing again. She tossed her shoulder bag onto the bed. Except for her sketchbook and felt pens, it was filled with stuff for the girl—a blanket, Pampers, a pacifier, and formula. "Formula is safer than breastfeeding, given your history of drug use," the nurse had warned. Maggie was surprised to discover that, even when her boobs hurt, she liked the intimacy, the feeling of connection and warm contentment that breastfeeding brought her.

She settled into the armchair and pulled up her blouse. The infant settled her tiny mouth on a nipple and sucked, gurgling with satisfaction like an addict getting her fix. Maggie closed her eyes and bit her lip. Her breasts were tight and painful today. The chair's thick silver threads scratched like sandpaper. When the feeding was over, she settled the baby onto the bed, and lay next to her. She closed her eyes, and before long, the boulevard's traffic noise hushed into a distant lullaby.

She's sitting cross-legged with strangers gathered around a fire in an abandoned warehouse. The flames illuminate their faces, some worn and ruined, grotesque in the flickering firelight. Others are young, but haggard and dead-eyed. There's an acrid reek in the air. The pipe passes from hand to hand, mouth to mouth. She waits, shaking and jonesing for a hit. She needs to zone out and be taken away from this world. The man sitting next to her offers a toothless grin and gropes her breast before handing the pipe over. Two hits, and she is flying—

A faint knocking sound seemed to come from a distance. She was being pulled away from the dream. She tried to put the distraction out of her head, but the knocking became louder and more insistent.

"Maggie? Are you in there? It's Brian."

She shook herself into consciousness. The baby was still asleep, her fat brown fingers curled into tiny fists. Standing unsteadily, she pulled down her blouse and smoothed her hair before opening the door. Brian stood on the other side, dressed like a hip troubadour in a bright-colored shirt and tight-fitting pants. He held a bouquet of white and lavender flowers.

"You look like someone's bridesmaid," she said.

Her brother laughed at the joke. "The flowers are for you."

Brian gazed at her intently. She wondered what he was looking for. Signs of drugs, or maybe demonic possession?

Carl stood behind him. "Nice place you chose to meet us," he said.

She was tempted to slam the door. Frowning at her brother, she complained, "I thought it was just going to be you."

"Carl and I decided that it might be best if we both came."

"I wish you had warned me. I would have worn armor."

He shot her one of those can't-we-all-just-get-along looks. But once inside the door, he kissed her on the forehead and enveloped her in a hug. Her irritation gave way to pleasure, her brother's warm arms calming her.

The baby was wide awake now, staring at the figures standing in the light from the open door.

Brian gasped. "There she is. Can I hold her?"

"Whatever. If you want to."

Her brother bent down and brought the baby up to his chest in a single elegant move. She emitted a gasp of surprise and wonder. Carl stood to one side attempting to muster a smile.

Brian gently pulled on the baby's fingers. "What's her name? You haven't said."

"She's Jane. Baby Jane." She couldn't take credit for naming the child. One of the nurses had suggested it, explaining that it was her mother's name.

"Jane. I like it," he affirmed. "She's beautiful, just like her mother."

Was beautiful. A lifetime ago.

Carl cleared his throat, looking uncomfortable. Brian pulled the blanket around Jane and handed the infant back to her. "Can we sit down and talk?"

"If you want." She'd ask them to leave if things got too difficult.

Her brother settled on the edge of the bed, patting the faded floral bedspread for her to sit next to him. Carl, looking like a talk show host, took the armchair across from them. She had to admit that he was good-looking. He had a good build. And that shiny dark hair, and thick eyebrows accentuating those pretty brown eyes.

"I've been doing a lot of thinking," said Brian, "and now that Carl and I are married—"

"You're married?" she asked. "You never told me that. When did that happen?"

"We thought it was best to wait to tell you until things had stabilized."

"Yeah, I know. You wanted to keep your fucked-up little sister out of the picture because she might ruin your wedding."

"That's not true, Maggie. You disappeared on me. No phone. No address."

That must have been when she had found out that she was pregnant. She was so royally messed up back then.

"Brian was worried about you," declared Carl.

I bet you told my only brother that it was best to forget about me, she thought. The baby grew antsy in her arms. No way she was going to bare her breasts in front of these two. She pulled a bottle of formula from her bag as Jane, red faced, yowled.

"Sometimes, I think she doesn't like me very much."

"Nonsense," said Brian. "You're her mother." Even so, he took Jane into his arms and brought her to his shoulder, patting her back gently.

"I'll warm the formula for you," Carl volunteered, placing the bottle in the microwave and studying the buttons. After testing the formula on his wrist, he handed the bottle to Brian, who inserted it into the infant's mouth.

They must have taken a gay parenting class, she thought, practicing with one of those weird lifelike dolls. She imagined the sketch she would make picturing the four of them— a fucking holy family for the twenty-first century.

Things came so easily for her brother. A nice apartment in West Hollywood. A job designing something on computers. Even a husband, to complete the picture. She bet Mr. Show Host treated Brian like gold.

"You two need to talk," said Carl. "I can take Jane."

The baby didn't even whimper as she was handed over.

Brian glanced at his husband. "Carl and I have been talking about this…and well, I'll get to the point. We have an extra bedroom at home, and we'd like to help you out with Jane."

They want to take my child away, she thought. Like Child Protective Services. A kind of blind panic, that old feeling of her autonomy being stolen, possessed her. She jerked away from his hand on her shoulder.

"Don't think you're fucking going to take her from me! I

give Jane all the attention she needs."

Brian spoke calmly. "I'm not saying you don't, Maggie, but she'll need a lot of things—doctor visits, clothes, and toys. You'll have more time for yourself that way. You could even start painting again."

"So, we could be one big happy dysfunctional family like before?"

"I know you got the worst end of things at home. What Dad did to you—"

"I don't want to talk about it!" A rush of static began to invade her head.

"You're my sister, Maggie. I want to keep you safe."

Now you want to protect me, she thought. Memories of her brother cowering under their father's swinging arms flooded her head. She remembered how often she ran to him, sobbing and fearful. He only sometimes defended her. He had taken his share of blows though too, especially after Dad discovered that his son was queer.

The old man was out of the picture now, no longer a terror.

She turned to Carl. "What about you?"

Brian opened his mouth to speak, but Carl cut him off by raising his dark eyebrows. "To be honest, when Brian first brought up the idea, I thought, holy shit! I married Brian, not his sister. Maybe I've made a mistake."

Brian shot him a surprised look.

"I admit that I wasn't exactly thrilled with the idea at first. But since it's what Brian wants, I'm willing to give it a try."

At least he's being honest. That was all she wanted from people. Not hiding behind words and gestures that seem like one thing, but mean another.

Her brother opened his arms to hug her. "I know it's a lot to take in."

She wasn't about to go all soft and agreeable. "You'd be making a big mistake!"

"That's a chance we're willing to take. If it isn't working for all of us, we'll come up with another solution. Together."

She walked to the window and parted the curtains. It was already growing dark outside. The motel's manager stood in front of the office, shooing away a homeless man who wheeled a shopping cart and was shouting his lungs out. A bottle flew from the man's hands and smashed against the asphalt.

Don't throw the baby out with the bathwater.

She swept Jane from Carl's lap and kissed her. She was tired of pretending to be tough. "You two have no idea what you're getting into."

Brian's eyes brightened. "Does that mean a yes?"

"I think your sister just agreed," declared Carl. "Let's get out of this dump."

Brian slipped the kit bag over his shoulder and led Maggie, with Jane in her arms, to the car. Carl took the driver's seat. A few raindrops scattered across the windows.

They pulled out of the driveway onto Hollywood. "We should stop on the way home and pick up some Pampers," said Brian. "Maybe some more formula."

He turned to her. "Anything else you can think of, Maggie?"

"I can't just leave the halfway house without permission. I need to return tomorrow."

"I know. We'll take you back in the morning and plead our case. It might take a while before they release you. There will be interviews and paperwork. But we'll work it out."

The rain came down harder, flooding the windows and making everything outside blurry. She closed her eyes and held

Jane tightly, imagining what it would be like to sleep in a nice bed for a change.

BROTHER IN THE RAIN

Mr. Motel Man tells me to get lost. Thinks he can buy me. Two dollars gets me shit. And now, like clockwork, it's raining pigs and chickens.

Hollywood off the 101. Ground Zero. Star-fucking billboards and dead palm trees. Spare Change, sad-assed hound, laying on my blanket. Wearing my silver sombrero and white-lace red tennies. Drivers pretend I'm *The Invisible Man.*

That's right, bro. I'm standing here just to ruin your day!

Damn rain in la-la land comin' down like rivers from sweet Jerusalem. Brothers and sisters lining up at the shelters. Strung-out dudes running for cover. Not me! I don't give up.

It's pouring. Rain, rain. Go the fuck away. The old man's snoring. This is hella boring.

Hey, tightwad ass in your seat! Cat got your wallet?

Saint Anthony of lost things scored me a miracle. Construction shed behind Sunset up-your-face Inn. Illegals come and go like rain. They don't bother me. Like Motel Man threatenin' me with 911 on his fucking flip phone. Thinking his driveway is a private red carpet for the one percent.

Hey! Windows closed, warming those toes. You don't give a flying fuck, do you?

Get my pints from the Lebanese. Symbionese is more like it. Steel bars on the mini-mart's windows

So-called social worker drills my head. Parasite informant for the super class.

I'm not taking any of your brain-drain drugs!

Mc D's. Burger King. KFC. Conspiracy to Make Americans Fatter Again. This ain't Spago, lady. You'd stink too if you were me.

I know the goddamn law! I pay good money for your shitty coffee!

Billy T scabs the hayseeds down on Sunset. Pretends he's peace and freedom with his goddam vegan sign in rainbow colors. $$ FOR VEGGIES.

You're a fucking con, Billy! Bad karma, man. Terra no incognito.

Said I misquoted Latin. Told him he misquotes his diet.

Billy's got more bark than Spare Change. Told me that I need to go back to school. Too damn late. Even gringo sounds Spanish.

Hablo español. Soy pollo loco.

The DEA chased me to Mexico. Ran my sorry ass from the neighborhood. I'm coming back charged like Rocket Man just to piss them off.

Only time you'll catch me running is away from your face, bitch!

Brother went to college. Two-point-four kids and a big honkin' house. Collects cash like I collect insults. But he don't read the messages in the graffiti.

You hand me a freakin' five-spot Lincoln, you'll hear me recite the Gettysburg Address.

The FBI and NSA want to grab me by the balls. Smart phones, internet, and GPS right up my ass. They're corrupt. Can't even locate the Missing Persons Bureau.

That's right. Shake your head at me. You don't know jack shit, Jack!

Showed Billy T a picture of my brother.

"This ain't your brother, man. That picture you, Jimmy, when you was straight."

Billy brags he's on Facebook. No way, Jose. People would just hit delete. Breaks into cars, tells me begging is demeaning. People who leave their shit in plain sight deserve to lose.

They going to throw your bad cheatin' heart into the joint someday, Billy.

Billy acting like he owns this place.

Hey, don't fuck with me, Billy! No quid pro dough. This is my spot. Haul your sorry butt back to where the sun don't shine no more.

Spare Change is barking like there's a full moon.

Homely hombre in a government car from CIA. Maybe it's KGB. Black honky waving his dollar bill like he's directing the symphony.

I know what that is, government man. It's my death certificate!

Stoplight Brother laughs.

Don't screw with me, spook. You got glass in your pants.

Speeds off like he's got a date.

Kiss my ass! Taste my pint bomb, fucker! Joke's all over your nasty face!

THE WAGER

"Cash or credit card?" asked the manager.

Harvey peered at the man's nametag. Edward. The man was around his own age, in his fifties, with an apologetic fringe of hair on the sides and only a hirsute memory on top.

He took pride in his own full head of hair, which had turned salt-and-pepper a decade ago. He always kept it freshly barbered. Customers responded positively to a salesman who was well-groomed.

"American Express." He pulled out his wallet, sending a wad of lottery tickets falling onto the floor.

"That's a lot of Lotto," chuckled the manager.

"I guess I'm addicted," he admitted, a bit embarrassed. Traveling drummers like himself, whose profession always fluctuated between fortune and failure, were often married to gambling. Harvey kneeled to pick up the fugitive stubs and pushed them into his suit coat's pocket.

"Lotto is for suckers," declared the manager. "I have a contact who runs an offshore operation. It's riskier, but potentially much more profitable than odds posted on the online sites"

"What are we talking about?"

"You name it. Sports games, prizefights, horses, dogs, even the Miss America pageant." He lowered his voice as if his next comments were meant for Harvey's ears alone.

"The Fury-Bryan match in Vegas this weekend is the big

one. Fury is favored four to one, but my associate tells me that he'll go down in the third round. You can watch the match On Demand in your room."

"How much to get in?"

"A nickel. Five hundred minimum, plus a ten percent commission."

Harvey whistled under his breath. "I'd have to check on a few things first."

"The match is tomorrow night, Mr. Morris. All wagers need to be placed no later than noon tomorrow."

On the way to his room, Harvey made a quick mental calculation. His checking account was very thin. Orders from retailers had lagged lately. He'd been in the lingerie game for twenty years now, but itinerant salesmen like himself were becoming a threatened species. What with all the online competition these days, buyers were negotiating his wholesale prices down to near break-even numbers.

Opening the door, he detected a heavy odor of cigarettes and Pine-Sol. He considered marching back to the office and requesting a new room, but after a full day driving all over L.A. on appointments, he was too beat to complain.

He grabbed a short rest. After showering and shaving, he stopped by the office. The manager, with a drink in hand, sat at his desk, looking overwhelmed by the heap of papers piled on its surface.

"You can put me in for a dime. You can use my American Express."

"Sorry, Mr. Morris. All wagers have to be in cash."

"Call me Harvey. I'll have it for you by tomorrow."

He drove out onto the boulevard. The motel's flickering neon sign reflected against the hood of his decade-old, immaculately maintained Lexus.

He needed to come up with a thousand in cash by tomorrow. The buyer from Playmates had called earlier and cancelled their appointment. Rampage claimed that their check was in the mail. Even Frederick's of Hollywood, his bread and butter, was late in paying the last invoice. He might still be able to catch the buyer at Sensations, the new 24/7 adult emporium on Gower Street. It always seemed to be crowded, catering to tourists and all the club kids who poured into Hollywood on the weekends.

The young clerk at Sensation's front desk sported multiple piercings and spiked hair. Slumped over the front counter, he appeared annoyed at being interrupted from flirting with an equally young customer. "The buyer isn't in," he sniffed, and snidely remarked, "You need to get with the program, grandpa. We order all our inventory online."

He was tempted to take one of their Made in China dildos and shove it up the kid's skinny ass. Instead, he stalked out and headed to the Denny's on Sunset. He preferred a quality steakhouse, of course, but he intended to make good on his wager. After a regrettable dinner of salty pot roast, gluey mashed potatoes and overcooked peas, he decided to stop for a good stiff drink.

Harvey drove to Sunset Junction and found a parking spot directly in front of the bar. A lucky sign. Nappers was one of the last holdouts from gentrification in the neighborhood. Its 1960s façade, adorned with faux driftwood planking and porthole windows, featured a nautical theme. He popped the trunk and retrieved his sample case. The yeasty odor of beer greeted him even before he reached the door. Cigarette smoke wafted from inside, testifying to the bar customers' insurgency against state smoking bans.

He settled onto a stool, the stiff cracked leather pinching his ass, and placed his sample case next to it. A grizzled veteran named Ben had presided here since he first discovered this place, but tonight, a lean youngster wearing a black T-shirt and jeans stood behind the bar. His back was turned away from his customers as he chattered on his phone in a low voice. Light from the screen illuminated his scruffy face and mass of curly dark hair.

Harvey cleared his throat, then picked up a bowl of peanuts from the counter and let it drop with a thud. The kid ended his call and plunked down a wet cocktail napkin. "What'll you have?" he drawled.

"I thought you'd never ask," growled Harvey, still bristling from his encounter with that juvenile at Sensations. "Maker's Mark, double. Neat."

The bartender pulled at his incipient goatee. "There's an awesome artisanal whiskey you should try. It's crafted in Brooklyn and distilled in small, curated batches."

He had no idea what the kid was talking about, but it certainly sounded like the beginning of the end for this neighborhood bar. "Thanks, but I'll stick with my order."

The bartender shot him a barely disguised look of disdain.

Harvey focused on the flotilla of bottles shelved on the wall. The mirror behind reflected his face. Despite the slight whittling away the years had accomplished, he still possessed a commanding forehead and forceful jaw, features that had once helped him achieve record-breaking sales. Those were great times. He felt on top of the world then.

But with the Fury-Bryan match occupying his thoughts, he turned to assess the bar's patrons. To his right, two beat-up, gray-haired guys were hunched on their stools and nursing their drinks. On his left, at a table near the door, a Latino-looking couple in their forties chatted animatedly. Across the way, a lonely-looking young man bent over the jukebox and studied its selections as Patsy Cline's voice wailed "I Fall To Pieces." In the back, the crack of cue balls from two men playing pool produced a staccato counter-rhythm to the music.

If he were to make good on that bet, he'd need to call Elizabeth and tell her that he was going to be late with the alimony payment again. Liz had wagered on a long shot when she married him. Years of being on the road, interrupted by brief reunions, had turned them into strangers. One fine spring day, she informed him that all bets were off between them. He should have seen it coming.

He signaled for a second shot.

The bartender whisked away his empty glass and replaced it with a refill. "Sorry I was so distracted earlier," he declared, and sighed. "Girlfriend issues."

Harvey sensed an opportunity. "You're having problems with your girlfriend?"

"She's always complaining that we don't spend enough quality time together. She gets royally pissed whenever I want to hang out with my buddies."

Harvey baited the hook. "The ladies certainly demand a lot of attention."

The young man nodded glumly. Harvey extended his arm across the bar.

"I'm Harvey Morris."

"I'm Jerrod." He elbow-bumped Harvey and picked up a towel to wipe a glass.

"Good to meet you, Jerrod. It's important to treat your lady well. The right gift can heal a lot of misunderstandings, let her know that you're thinking of her."

Casting the line.

"You mean, like flowers and shit?"

"Flowers are fine, but it's a win-win when you give her something that you will both enjoy." He winked.

The bartender gazed at him blankly. Bobber floating.

"What's your girlfriend's name, by the way?"

"Her name is Maya."

Harvey lowered his voice. "If I can ask a personal question. How *are* things with Maya? If you know what I mean."

"It's generally pretty awesome, at least when she's not totally pissed at me."

"I bet she appreciates it when you tell her that she's beautiful and sexy."

"She'll call me sexist, but I know she likes it."

"The term 'sexist' isn't in my vocabulary," said Harvey. "But sex is."

Tugging the line.

He lifted his sample case onto the top of the bar and popped its latch. "I have something that will put more juice into your sex life. Have you got a minute?"

Jerrod glanced around and nodded. "This place is dead tonight."

"These are special items that are guaranteed to smooth over any rough patches with Maya."

The young man's nose twitched at the pheromone-spiked scent floating from the case, leaning over the counter for a closer look inside.

Harvey pulled the case away ever so slightly. Luring his catch. "Is Maya a blond or a brunette?"

"She's Asian. She has really awesome long dark hair."

"Then I have just the thing for you." He dug past several diaphanous items before he found what he was looking for, a

V-shaped wedge of red nylon edged in black lace. "This is from my best-selling line. It's a G-string, even skimpier than a thong. A woman turns into a spitfire when she wears this. Go ahead. Feel it."

The bartender touched the filmy fabric warily, as if it might explode in his hands.

"Imagine how awesome Maya will look wearing this. She'll want to show it off to you."

The young man's phone was vibrating. Harvey needed to take charge, and told him to ignore it. He dug through more layers of lace, nylon, and spandex, pulling out a bra constructed of two quarter-moon, red lace cups edged with black lace. He displayed it like a matador waving a cape before a rutting bull.

"This is meant to be paired with the G-string." It's called the Hollywood Flirt.

The bartender stared at the contraption dubiously. "She doesn't usually wear a bra."

"This is for those special occasions, remember? Think of Maya's delight when she sees your awesome gifts. Imagine her, undressing and putting them on for you. She will probably want to do it right then."

Hook sinking.

Harvey noted the excited glimmer in the young man's eyes.

"You could bring them to her tonight."

The bartender hesitated, rubbing the stubble on his chin. "How much are they?"

"A lot less than you'd pay at regular retail. I'll let these go for eighty dollars. That includes a special gift box. You can surprise Maya after work, unless, of course, you're planning on getting together with your buddies."

Jerrod shook his head. "No way, man. Not tonight." He checked his wallet and consulted the tip jar. "I'm in, but some of it will have to be in singles."

Landing his catch.

"You won't be single much longer," joked Harvey, as he wrapped the items in silver tissue and placed then in a gold box with a lusty red bow.

Jerrod counted out the cash he had cobbled together. "Maya's been threatening to break up with me," he confided. "You just might have saved my ass."

He reached for a bottle on the top shelf and poured two fingers into a snifter. "This is the artisanal variety I told you about. It's on the house."

Harvey took a tentative sip. The Brooklyn-brewed bourbon was actually damn smooth.

He voiced his approval before turning his attention to the Latino couple. He noticed the couple had seemed curious about his wares.

The man, his hair cropped short and muscles rippling, wore a white tank top that revealed a collection of tattoos covering his arms and shoulders. His companion had poured herself into an impossibly tight, electric blue dress that rode high on her thighs.

Her face, half-hidden by a wig of mahogany curls, seemed drawn and a bit worn, but came to life as she laughed at something her date said. When he reached across the table to grab her hands, she pushed him away with an alluring smile.

Judging from their interplay, they were lovers, but not married. Harvey raised his glass in a salute. The tattooed boyfriend nodded back. The man's wallet was practically bulging from his pants pocket.

And what about that pudding-faced young man staring sadly into the jukebox? As he considered which customer to approach next, a very tall woman with broad shoulders came in through the door.

Jerrod poured him another, then got busy polishing glasses, humming to himself.

Happy, it seemed, about his prospects with Maya later tonight.

He sauntered into the office the next morning and handed his wager to the manager.

Edward raised his eyebrows at the small bills, but patiently counted out the cash and recorded it into a tattered notebook. "I'll call this in right now. A dime on Bryan, in three, right? You're watching the match tonight, no doubt."

Harvey smiled. "The first three rounds anyway."

"You're that confident, eh? I suppose you'll be checking out after you collect your winnings."

"I may stick around a couple more days. I made a few surprise sales last night. I think your motel is bringing me luck."

Harvey walked to his beloved Lexus, humming a pop song from Napper' jukebox that stuck in his head. He remembered the words to the refrain. "Can't Buy Me Love."

He had made an early reservation at Mastro's in Beverly Hills. He planned to knock back a couple of their classic martinis with his steak dinner before returning in time to see Bryan land his powerful uppercut, and make him a happy man.

REFUGE

Jack pulled the brim of his baseball cap down low over his forehead and stepped outside. The midafternoon sunlight reflecting against the motel's peeling pink paint assaulted him. He glanced at the hills, the Los Angeles smog blurring the landscape. Better to lose oneself in its democratic haze, he thought, than risk exposure under clear skies.

He had taken the room for its discreet location hidden from the street. He hadn't left it for three days, tuning in to the news on TV and ordering in—pizza from Vito's on La Cienega, corned beef and pastrami from Cantor's, alcohol and cigarettes delivered by the attractive son of the Syrian who owned the mini-mart around the corner. He had been tempted to call an escort service, but thought better of it.

Rubbing the stubble on his cheeks, he retreated inside and began to pace. His hands were greasy from that last piece of cold pizza, his T-shirt and sweatpants were stained. An upturned bottle of gin sat next to the ashtray filled with butts, a graveyard for the habit he thought he'd given up years ago.

How the mighty have fallen, his life in shambles, hiding out and lamenting his exile from favor like the biblical David. It was only days ago that he was perched on top of the world, lionized by the media, admired by his constituents.

Political royalty. Jack Hunt the state senator with national aspirations. His wife Carolyn the successful San Francisco attorney.

He realized that his rise in state politics was preordained, even though he chose a very different political path from his deep-dyed conservative father, the late U.S. Senator Sam Hunt. He had benefitted from a reformist wave, his first campaign for state assembly fueled by public outrage at Wall Street, big corporations and their highly-paid CEOs. Powerful interests opposed his run for state senator two years later, which he nevertheless won in a close election. He remembered the victory celebration that night with Carolyn at his side. There seemed to be no limit to his aspirations. U.S Congressman in four years, the Presidency in eight.

He was taken by surprise when the axe came down. Now, thinking back, he realized that privilege had blinded him to the pitfalls of public life. Things could turn on a dime, and they had.

Last Friday, *The Sacramento Bee* had published a front-page story that detailed his frequent use of certain personal services, including Boy Call, an escort service, and a male massage parlor. The report's last sentence was perhaps the most politically damaging: "Is Senator Hunt using taxpayer money to pay for male models, porn actors, and young men-for-hire?"

He found himself ensnared in a public shitstorm overnight. Reporters dogged him. Old allies didn't take his phone calls or respond to his texts. Some of his constituents called for him to step down.

He had called in his bewildered staff to handle damage control. A statement was issued. Senator Hunt does not deny that he used these services, but he assures all California taxpayers that he paid for them from his private account. The nature of these services was not addressed. That would come later, delaying the inevitable, providing another twenty-four hours to strategize.

Jack loved Carolyn and his kids, but even his district's liberal constituency would not view it that way. He might somehow survive the scandal of using certain services from men, but the image cultivated by him of devoted husband and family man would be viewed as hypocritical. He could not be trusted.

He couldn't reach Carolyn for forty-eight hours after the bombshell dropped. How much had she known? She must have been aware, standing by his side but saying nothing while his eyes locked onto a handsome man at a fundraiser or followed a waiter's practiced movements at a cocktail party.

He left the capital on Saturday night and drove to their home in Piedmont nestled in the Oakland hills. Fortunately, ten-year old Marcie and her brother David were spending two weeks with friends in Hillsborough across the bay. Carolyn finally appeared late Sunday morning, looking as tired and haggard as he was feeling after two sleep-deprived nights. But she was prepared to do battle, launching into him in a prosecutorial mode impressive even for her as a public prosecutor.

"You're a pathological liar, Jack. I don't really care about your damn voters. You've been living lies, and you've made me live with them, too."

Guilty as charged. Meeting her angry eyes were the most uncomfortable moments of the entire nightmare. "I'm truly sorry, Carolyn. I don't know what else to say."

"You're goddamned sorry. Is that really all you have to say? Apparently, your hunky speechwriter hasn't prepared a statement for me yet."

She said that she was there only to pack. She dashed upstairs and slammed the bedroom door. He threw the dregs of his coffee cup into the sink, and stared blankly out the window before climbing up the stairs and stopping at the landing, wondering what would happen to his family. He knocked. Carolyn sat on their bed against a pile of pillows with a phone at her ear. Sunlight streamed through the tall French windows, illuminating her auburn hair and shapely bare legs. Her eyes were red-rimmed, but she now appeared composed. He perched on the edge of the bed and attempted to take her hands, but she swatted him away.

Now staring at the empty bottle of gin, he recalled how powerless he had felt that morning. He had grown skillful at handling political crises, but was at a complete loss facing his wife. It was the same mute defenselessness he had experienced as a child whenever his father reproved him.

An hour later, he found her packing. "I need to return to Sacramento. I do love you, Carolyn." She glanced up and continued folding sweaters and skirts.

He barely remembered the drive back to Sacramento. His thoughts were disconnected and fragmented, as if his mind belonged to a stranger. He sped past a phalanx of media vans and clustered reporters that surrounded his apartment building and parked in the underground garage.

Carolyn and he were brutally honest with one another during a half dozen phone calls that Monday. He discovered that Carolyn knew that he must be having liaisons, and had also been unfaithful. They agreed to a temporary arrangement. Carolyn would remain with him publicly for the time it took to settle his political fate. "As far as I'm concerned, it's a political marriage anyway," she declared.

He realized that she needed to hurt him as he had hurt her. Still, she kept her word and stood stoically by his side at the press conference where he apologized to his constituents and supporters before announcing his resignation.

Carolyn made her own announcement. She was taking

Marcie and David to her parents' home in Wyoming. The next morning, he found a rental waiting for him in the underground garage. He had instructed a trusted aide to max-out several ATMs and purchase a prepaid cell phone. His credit cards and iPhone could be traced. He was now in burner phone territory, like the criminals Carolyn prosecuted.

A deep numbing sadness set in as he headed south on the I-5. The humiliating public exposure of those last few days had forced him to confront an episode he had tried to bury. He was fourteen. His cousin Jeremy was spending a week at his house. His father discovered them together in the pool house. Shaking with disbelief and anger, he ordered them both to dress. Later that afternoon, his father summoned Jack to his mahogany-walled office. He remembers quaking before the imposing desk as his father's eyes bore into him, with that same damning intensity he directed toward his political opponents.

"If I ever catch you, or hear of you again"—he cleared his throat—"in *that* regard, I will disown you. You're the son of Senator Hunt, and you will behave as one. Have I made myself perfectly clear?"

He had remained silent, a captive under his father's steely gaze, until he was dismissed. Rushing into his bedroom, he fell onto his bed, sobbing. His tears were not only from the shame of being discovered, but that he would forever be judged by his father's impossible standards.

He sometimes wondered what his life would have been like if he had told the Senator to go fuck himself. He may not have necessarily been any happier, but at least he would have lived authentically, rather than committing himself to perpetuating a lie.

How much longer could he hold out in this room?

He pulled out a photograph from his wallet. It had been taken at Lake Tahoe. The four of them standing on a dock, looking happy. He loved his family and would always. But he had pretended with them. That was his true disgrace.

Jack ordered another pack of cigarettes and a bottle of gin from the mini-market. It was growing dark outside. Several men, day-laborers by the look of them, were filing into the room closest to the street. More cars had appeared in the motel's parking court. Travelers needing a cheap room, coming from out of town.

His drive here had likely been more eventful than their trips.

He had stopped only once, to fill his tank at the Shell station in Buttonwillow. He was alarmed to see his face appear on the pump's video screen. A newscaster was reporting on "Mr. Hunt's relationships with numerous male prostitutes." Even the crawl at the bottom of the screen carried text of the scandal. His stomach lurched at a clip showing Carolyn and the kids being hustled through the PreCheck line at San Francisco International.

The reporter maintained a neutral expression as she related the details of the senator's transgressions, but he noted the trace of glee that shone in her eyes.

We're all hypocrites, he thought bitterly.

The broadcast echoed from all the surrounding pumps. He turned to see a woman pointing her phone at him, a parasite eager for her five minutes of fame. She would alert the media and bring the fucking bloodhounds. Choppers descending from over the Tehachapi Mountains. News vans converging from the north and the south to follow him.

Rage possessed him, anger at everyone who believed they owned a piece of him—his demagogic father, the relentless media, and the public savoring his fall from grace.

"You bitch!" he shouted, as he sprinted toward the entitled snoop. He grabbed her phone and opened it to remove the SIM card before tossing both into the dry brush beyond.

He retreated to his car as she screamed obscenities. Peeling away to turn onto the freeway, he heard the pump's nozzle break away from his car. His act of catharsis was worth the price of more public evidence of his degradation.

The sulfuric sunset to the west had turned obscenely beautiful, the clouds blood red against a sky of brooding purple.

He had watched for any signs of being followed as he ascended the Grapevine, until at last, he was lost in the San Fernando Valley's heavy traffic. For only this one moment on his drive south had he considered ending it, driving his rental off the steep side of the road into a power post.

His funeral would no doubt be very well attended.

He laughed darkly at the irony of being back at the Sunset Inn after so many years. He had attended numerous star-studded events in L.A. but he hadn't set foot on Hollywood Boulevard for many years, not since taking an innocuous, seedy motel room here for a rendezvous with a callboy. Even though the light from the sky had faded, he pulled down his cap and put on sunglasses before entering the office, where the blue light from a TV flickered.

The manager had appeared unfazed when he paid in cash for a three-night stay. The motel must get a lot of sketchy cash-only customers, he imagined, among whose ranks he now belonged. This morning, he informed the man that he planned to stay for a few more days.

He hadn't shaved or showered since checking in. He flipped on the bathroom light and gazed at the disheveled reflection he saw in the mirror. His always-winning smile was missing, the normally confident eyes veiled. The image made him think of a mug shot for a criminal on the run. His rap sheet was relatively short, but his celebrity had made him the object of a statewide manhunt.

"They want my ass for liking ass," he joked, his face in the mirror suddenly appearing more Jack the Ripper than Jack Hunt.

He stripped off his grubby T-shirt and sweatpants, and jumped into the shower.

The warm water soothed him, washing away the stress of the past days. After toweling himself down, he shrugged into a black polo and jeans. He wasn't going to shave. He was tired of shaving, usually twice a day to look spruce for speeches and appearances, meetings and fundraisers, for all the Q &A's with constituents.

He wouldn't order in again. Instead, he drove to Silver Lake, found a quiet restaurant, and enjoyed a good meal. He didn't go out of his way to be inconspicuous. He was tired of hiding. They would find him eventually, anyway.

The prospect of returning to that dismal motel room set him on edge. He decided to drive to West Hollywood. Even in his casual clothes and cap, the men cruising and carousing on Santa Monica recognized him. He was on every news feed. A few nodded and even smiled, most gawked. He was big news, after all. He shot them all a wry, weary look, as if to say, "Yeah, I know. My career is now in the toilet. My old life is dead."

Sometime after midnight, while sitting at the bar in one the clubs, a dark-haired young man approached him hesitantly, as if considering whether it was the right thing to do.

"Excuse me. Aren't you…"

"Yes. I am. Why don't you sit down? May I buy you a drink?"

MOTHS

A car turned into the driveway, its engine sputtering and pinging. Edward took pride at guessing the make, and even the year, of the guests' vehicles by sound alone. But when the car came to a stuttering stop in the parking court, his eyebrows raised at the sight of an old Buick Regal, its original royal blue color faded almost to white in spots and rust blooming in uneven patches across its doors.

A short, stocky man emerged from the driver's seat. He wore black dress pants and a spotless white guayabera shirt. He gazed about him with a combination of guarded wariness and mannered self-confidence. His dark face was strong and broad, with cheekbones that were deeply chiseled.

He looked like a carved figure from some Mayan temple, thought Edward.

A slim woman slid from the passenger seat and blinked into the bright light. Her black hair was parted in the center; a thick braid coiled in the back. She smoothed her loose white dress decorated with colorful embroidery on the hem and neckline. A shaft of sunlight touched her shoulders, which seemed to make her glow.

Rara avis. A term Edward thought he picked up from one of those late-night nature programs he often fell asleep to.

The couple entered the office quietly, as if determined to disturb not even a mote of dust.

"Sir, we would like a room." The man enunciated his words

carefully and formally as if he had practiced this simple request.

The woman was older than Edward had first thought, but her dark hair and fine features were even more striking up close. The man was one lucky son of a bitch. A lewd thought passed through his head, but he quickly focused on the business at hand.

"For how many nights?" he asked.

"For tonight and tomorrow night," said the man.

"We were married today," the woman explained.

"Congratulations. Welcome to the Sunset Inn. We don't have a honeymoon suite, but Room 7 is available."

"How much does it cost?" asked the man.

"Eighty-nine dollars per night. Are you paying in cash or with a credit card?"

"Cash."

Edward might normally be tempted to pocket the second night's rate. But then again, the accountant's visit was fast approaching. He offered the couple an offer that would salve his guilty conscience. "Since it's your honeymoon, I can give you the second night at half-price. With tax, that will be $156."

The groom appeared perplexed.

Edward assumed his confusion was due to a language barrier, and explained in his pidgin Spanish. "You pay *cincuenta y seis dólares for dos noches.*"

The man uttered, "*Gracias,*" and pulled out his wallet to reveal a thick wad of bills. Holy Jesus, thought Edward. He could be a drug dealer, a runner for a cartel who drove that beater to stay under the radar. He almost regretted his decision to offer a discount.

"It's dangerous to carry so much cash around," warned Edward. "We don't have safes in the rooms, but you're welcome to use the safe in the office."

"No, *gracias*." The man shot him a shrewd look before swiftly counting out bills like a dealer doling out cards at a blackjack table.

Edward avoided the man's gaze as he handed him a pen. "You just need to sign your name here."

The man printed his name—Antonio Ortiz—in bold block letters.

He handed the room key to his guests, glancing at the wife, and wishing them a nice stay.

Ortiz held the door for his bride and opened the Regal's trunk, big enough to stash a body with room to spare. The woman followed him to the room and the door closed behind them.

Edward wondered if it might be opened again so they could perform the usual ceremony. I guess they don't carry the bride across the threshold where he's from, he thought. Or maybe he's just saving his energy.

He poured two fingers of whiskey, slumped into his chair and clicked the remote. The TV was tuned to a channel he had been watching the night before. It now featured a program filmed in the highlands of some country in Central America. A spiderlike creature possessing fierce-looking tentacles covered with spiky hairs creeped toward a pale white moth. The spider struck swiftly, grasping its victim with engorged tentacles. The narrator announced that they released poisonous venom to paralyze their prey into helplessness. Edward watched as the moth frantically fluttered its wings before collapsing. The spider carried its victim away and consumed all of it except for its scaley, powdery wings, which floated to the ground.

His thoughts turned to his newest guests, the stalwart husband and his slender bride. They appeared happy, but he noticed a certain sadness in their eyes.

He wondered if those spiders were native to the country they had come from.

Antonio lay on the motel's bed, staring at the thin ray of light that leaked through the half-closed bathroom door. Behind it, Rosalia was changing out of her wedding dress.

He recalled the first time they had met, only a year ago at the Romero's July 4th fiesta. He had worked with Benito Romero at construction sites all over Southern California. The work paid well, better than the pickup jobs he had taken when he first arrived here. He was saving money.

The Romero's American holiday celebration included dishes from home, including his favorite, deep-fried *buñuelos*. As he listened to the high piping strains of the music accompanied by a tong drum, he scanned the guests for any unwelcome faces from the past. This was when he first noticed Rosalia. She was of pure Indigenous stock like himself. Her observant brown eyes were set off by thick dark hair and eyebrows. He recognized something familiar in her downcast but determined expression.

Benito told him that she had just arrived from back home and was staying with them. Rosalia had left her daughter in her mother's care until she could bring her here safely. Antonio understood. Guatemala was becoming nearly as dangerous as it had been during the civil war. Violent gangs had replaced murderous government troops.

Felicia Romero introduced them, and he asked her to dance. Before the party's end, he realized that even though they had both suffered from the war, their separate experiences of it could either pull them apart or bind them together.

During a lunch break that next week, he asked Benito what

he knew about his house guest's life during the conflict. His friend related an incident.

Rosalia had been sleeping when government soldiers entered her village just before dawn. They shouted obscenities, kicked down doorways, and dragged occupants to stand outside their homes. Men were separated from the women and children, and were ordered to dig a long, deep hole. The women wailed and hurled curses. After the men finished, they were ordered to line up in front of the hole. The terrified voices of the women grew louder as shots from the soldiers' rifles echoed through the steep hills surrounding the village. The troops tied the older boys together with ropes, and did the same with some of the girls. Others were stripped and raped. Rosalia's brothers were among those who were taken away.

The entire village was torched and burned to the ground by nightfall.

"Was Rosalia one of the girls who was assaulted?" asked Antonio, trying to mask his apprehension.

"She managed to escape with her mother into the jungle, but there was nothing for them to return to. Their life had been stolen away. They moved to the capital with some of the other women."

He had tried to maintain an impassive expression during Benito's account, but his own sequestered memories were still poison inside him, one he wished he could release. His older brothers were among *los desaparecidos*, disappeared in the war's massacres. He escaped that fate but was forced to march by the government's soldiers who kept shouting, *"Rapido! Rapido,"* until his feet bled. He was convinced they were taking him to a secret place to kill him. Instead, he was made to work for the troops, fetching water and cleaning their boots and uniforms, stealing chickens from farms. Until, one day, they told him that he was old enough, and made him a boy soldier.

The memory of his first raid would always remain captive in his mind. Gunshots greeted the dawn's orange light. Dwellings were torched, the occupants separated.

"All males over fourteen must be executed," ordered the sergeant.

Antonio was shaking. Warm piss dribbled down his thighs.

"Kill them, or you will join them," growled the officer.

He did what he was ordered to do, forcing the heads of boys his own age under water to save bullets, pouring gasoline on dead bodies and burning them. This hell continued for more than two years until, one day, the government decided to end its campaign. He was cast away, no longer needed and with no place to land.

Drinking cervezas with Benito after work that day, he confessed. "I came here to forget, to erase the past, but I know that is impossible."

His friend looked away. "We've all been touched by the war. You did what you had to do to survive."

Until he met Rosalia, Antonio believed that the war had canceled his ability to feel anything but regret. He confessed to her, and she understood. They had both been ensnared by a power much stronger than themselves. He discovered that being with her calmed his soul, and perhaps even promised a fresh beginning.

After the wedding, the Romeros hosted a party, a community celebration. Music and food. Everyone danced. Guests stuffed money into a basket for the couple. Together, they would bring Rosalia's daughter here.

Now sitting on the bed, Antonio waited for Rosalia. At last, she appeared and walked lightly toward him. Her form seemed to shimmer in the room's dim light, the same luster that he sometimes saw glowing from the pale moths on moonlit nights in the highlands back home.

"*La tierra prometida*," she whispered, raising her arms in joy like wings.

"Yes, our own promised land," he replied, wrapping his large hands around her waist and pulling her gently toward him. She accepted his invitation as if it was the most natural thing in the world. They embraced, holding one another before any of the old darkness might close in on them.

CHAPEL OF LOVE

Edward ran a hand across his sweaty forehead. A chill of dread overtook him. He was failing to reconcile the motel's books. He had been sloppier than usual these last six months, and the numbers he invented didn't work. Even the meager winnings he had replaced for the funds he had taken shouted that all bets were off.

He was certain the petty thefts that kept adding up would bring him down this time. His addiction to drink and gambling was like a politician's craving for crack and call girls. But instead of leaving office as a well-paid lobbyist or political pundit, he might very well leave this office for a long stretch in prison.

At first, he believed he could replace the borrowed cash from his winnings, but this bet hadn't exactly panned out. He should have stopped long ago.

A car roared into the entrance and hurled into the parking court, interrupting his brooding. A metallic red Mustang, a beefed-up a Boss 302. Its overwrought V8 engine gunned pulsing assaults, pounding the office walls and rattling the windows. The young driver sprang out, his pudding face full of confidence and topped by a thatch of sandy-colored hair. His navy-blue polo shirt, khaki pants, and boaters marked him as a suburbanite.

The kid entered the office like a shot, drumming his fingers on the front desk's worn counter. "Anyone home? I need a room."

A privileged idiot, thought Edward, rising slowly from his desk and glaring at the intruder. He perused the register, pretending to look for a vacancy. "I don't believe we have a room available right now."

The kid stared out at the nearly empty lot. "I suppose all your guests must come on foot, then."

Cute. "I'll need to see your driver's license first."

The kid scoffed, pulled out his wallet and flashed his ID. Gill Everson. Nineteen years old. A Thousand Oaks address.

Edward eyed the Mustang's passenger busy adjusting her face in the visor's mirror. She was disagreeably familiar. "How old is she?"

"I've only had it for a couple months."

"I'm talking about the girl inside."

The young man's voice quavered slightly. "She's…my age."

"You must share the same babysitter, then." He couldn't help the sarcasm. After a miserable morning pouring over the accounts, he was taking pleasure in ruffling this fledgling's feathers.

Whose baby face was flushing bright red under his bottle tan. "I could always take my business elsewhere, you know," he answered, his foot knocking against the front desk with impertinence. "I could report you for discrimination too."

Edward laughed. "On what grounds?"

"Ageism, or … The kid's eyes shot up, searching for another fraudulent category.

Edward decided to end the duel, and raised his hands in mock defeat. "I found a room for you. It's eighty bucks."

Gill Everson opened his wallet and took out a credit card, but then he hesitated and laid four twenties on the counter before adding two tens to the pile, along with a lick of sarcasm. "The extra is for all your trouble."

The kid was arrogant, but not stupid. His parents probably supply him with a credit card. They would have discovered the motel stay when they received the next statement.

"It's Room 8, directly across the parking court. The laundry will be running in the service room next door for the rest of the afternoon. I hope you won't mind the noise."

His newest check-in shot him an amused look. "I don't think we'll be bothered by any noise."

He grabbed the key from Edward's hands and rushed from the office. Gesticulating excitedly to his passenger, he gunned the Mustang's engine as if he were at Indy 500's starting line, and coasted a full twenty feet to park in front of the room.

"Christ!" muttered Edward. "You'd think at his age he could manage to walk."

He watched the kid's questionable date step from the car and lean provocatively against the passenger door. She wore skintight jeans slit at the knees, a navel-ring baring top, and a hardened expression. The bright afternoon sun wasn't doing her blond dye job any favors, her hair as yellow as the uneaten banana that lay on his office desk.

She was one of the regulars. Her name was Crystal, Tiffany or Jolene, depending on the day of the week. The kid bounded around the car like some favored puppy, that image quickly erased when he pressed his groin against her. The girl took him by the arm and led him toward the door and to a hastily promised pleasure.

Edward shook his head and muttered, "She'll eat him for lunch."

Gil Everson strutted into the office late the next morning. His hair was wet and his polo shirt hung loosely outside his rumpled khakis. The kid was as jumpy as a windup toy and he was grinning broadly, as if advertising a secret that he couldn't keep.

Edward glanced up from his desk "You can leave the key on the counter."

"You won't believe the night I just had," the kid yelped. His pupils were dilated.

"Let me guess. You thought you had picked up a girl, but she was actually a guy. And you had a great time together anyway."

"Ha, ha. Very funny. Suzanne told me that I was the greatest she had ever been with. And she wants to see me again and again." He winked in case his meaning wasn't entirely clear.

So, her name was Suzanne this time. A fresh start with a freshman. Edward pulled his chair from his desk with a screech. "This isn't my business, but I'll give you a pointer. Suzanne, or whatever she's calling herself, will tell you anything as long as she sees your green."

Everson shot him an offended look. He pulled out his wallet. "I'm paying for another night."

"It's Friday. We're completely booked."

The kid looked momentarily stumped by the news, but quickly pulled himself together. "I want to show you something."

He foisted his phone in front of Edward's face. Its screen revealed the image of a smarmy looking man with slicked-back hair and wearing a flashy green suit. The kid scrolled through several more shots of what appeared to be a living room that had been ginned up to resemble a chapel, complete with a pulpit framed by urns filled with plastic flowers. A red carpet separated two ornate pews. The last was a shot of the exterior with a sign over the entrance—Hollywood Chapel of Love.

Gil Everson stashed the phone in his pants pocket. "All you

need to get married is an ID and two hundred bucks. Suzanne told me about it."

"You're kidding, of course." Edward thought he had seen and heard everything here over the years, but this was a first. "Your virginity wasn't the only thing you lost last night."

"Suzanne is not what you think. She's had a tough life."

"Tough life, tough woman. That's her gig. Don't be a fool."

He recalled his own stupidity at that age. He had driven into Cincinnati one night and picked up a hooker downtown. He paid her forty dollars for a quickie on the front seat. Later, they shared a joint. The girl told him that he was special. She wanted to see him again. The following weekend, he searched up and down Vine Street, and discovered her on a side street. She was leaning into the open window of an idling car. He watched as she opened the passenger door and disappeared inside.

He hoped Everson's obsession would disappear as quickly as his own had. The kid could be thumbing his nose at his parents and might move on to something else. He had been rebellious too at that age, but look where it got him.

"I can see that you're high right now. What did she give you? I'm sure Suzanne performed very well and must be very convincing, even with a smart kid like you. Pay her double if you feel you need to, and then wish her goodbye."

"That's not what—

"Go back to Santa Barbara where you belong. Find a nice girl and get married at Cathedral Peak and have your reception at your dad's golf club Your parents won't disown you then. Meanwhile, ditch the girl. I'll extend your stay until midafternoon, and you can sleep off the high before you return."

A momentary look of rebellion clouded the kid's face, but

then he seemed to comprehend. He shrugged and slammed the office door behind him.

Suzanne was waiting for him in her halter top and calf-choking jeans. The slanting morning light coarsened her features. The two talked, first in low voices, but then louder in argument. He handed her a fistful of bills and then attempted to kiss her. Angry, she pushed him away and retreated out to the street clutching her purse.

The kid, looking forlorn, peered through the office windows. Edward pointed to his room across the parking court.

Late that afternoon, Gil Everson returned to the office. "I owe you thanks for saving my ass. I don't know what I was thinking."

"You weren't thinking, that's all. Now get out of here. We need to clean your room before tonight's rush."

Minutes later, the Mustang peeled away, leaving a furious patch of rubber on the asphalt. Gil Everson smacked his horn twice, an irritating Thank you, before traffic noise from the Boulevard silenced the car's lusty roar.

That evening, Edward stepped out to buy a bottle of scotch. He spotted the girl across the street, gazing at her reflection in the Starlet Club's blackened windows. Suzanne, or maybe it was Tiffany tonight, smoothed her hair and adjusted her skimpy top before stepping to the curb, intent on business.

BAMBOO

Bao Nguyen tossed the banh mi sandwich his mother had packed for him into the room's mini fridge. Rail thin, and though approaching middle age, the wisp of dark hairs above his upper lip had not yet felt the steel of a blade. Settling onto a chair, he ignored the No Smoking sign posted on the motel room's door and enjoyed a forbidden cigarette, blowing vaporous rings toward the dim light that leaked from a tattered lampshade.

The dark blue suit that Bao's mother, Mai Nguyen, had insisted he wear hung in the closet next to a starched white shirt. A bright green tie draped over it, like a shiny Con Long dragon.

"First impressions are most important," declared Mai, "even to a simple country girl like her."

His mother reminded him daily that he must get married before she died. Her imminent death was her a favorite topic, followed by the stories of surviving wartime famine and American carpet bombings. She also loved telling him how she had endured a dangerous sea journey with her infant son in order to provide a better life for him.

"We must find a good wife for you soon!" she might shout from the restaurant's kitchen as Bao set the tables.

"There's plenty of time for that," he always retorted, even when she reminded him that he was nearly forty.

When he refused to consider the pampered daughters of her two *Tiến lên* card-playing friends, his mother decided to undertake a modern approach. She recruited a customer to help with her matrimonial campaign, a regular customer who always brought his laptop with him to the restaurant as a companion. Bao heard them conspiring, embarrassed that his mother was divulging personal information he'd rather not want to share with strangers. Several bad photographs soon appeared on a Vietnamese matchmaking site, including one of him as a naked toddler, his face buried in a bowl of pho.

The stilted description of his attributes was terribly dull, he thought, but he hoped it would discourage response: *Bao is a nice-looking American Vietnamese. He is industrious and responsible and desires to marry a smart, hardworking Vietnamese girl.*

He had his own interpretation of the posting: *Dominating mother of an illegitimate mongrel who works for her like a slave seeks another submissive slave who will provide her with a grandson.*

"We will find a nice girl from a village," Mai assured him. She believed that nothing had changed back home since she had left. To her, people there still lived without running water and electricity, walked or used bicycles to go places and passed water buffalos wandering through muddy streets.

"We are in the twenty-first century," he reminded his mother, "not in your memories of Vietnam." The country was prosperous now. Remote villages had Wi-Fi and mobile service. Hanoi and Ho Chi Minh City were filled with skyscrapers, and vehicles competed for space on congested streets, just like in Los Angeles.

Fortunately, his mother's posting received very few replies. None of them passed her scrutiny, never mind his opinion. Just as she was about to abandon the Web as "no good for getting married," a distant cousin in Vietnam responded, claiming that her twenty-two-year-old daughter was "pretty, smart, and very industrious." Photos revealed a rather plain young woman with alert brown eyes. Her name was Truc, which meant bamboo.

"A fortunate name," declared Mai Nguyen. "She will bend with the wind," No doubt, she was already putting the girl to work in the restaurant.

Bao bent with the wind himself when he agreed to exchange messages with this industrious cousin. Truc's command of English was surprisingly good. Before long, they were spending time talking on Skype.

She was earnest and determined, and spoke honestly. "I want to marry an American, so I can escape my controlling parents once and for all."

If he married a woman seeking independence, he thought, that might help him to seek his own. When he told his mother his decision, she nearly dropped a pan of grilled cha ca on the floor, and then embraced him.

"I've prayed for this every day. You've made me happy, *con trai.*"

A few days before Truc was scheduled to arrive, Bao announced that he wanted to meet her alone. "The morning drive to the airport is terrible, so I've decided to stay in town overnight."

His mother appeared stunned that he didn't want her to share in the welcome.

"Don't waste the money," she objected. "Save it for your bride."

"I want to be well rested so that I can make a good impression, like you said."

She scowled, but nodded in agreement. "Flowers at the airport are not fresh and too expensive. Buy them from a street vendor."

He could stay much closer to the airport, but he planned to spend the night in Hollywood, where he once cruised the boulevard with his high school friends on weekends. They tried to pick up girls, but they never succeeded. This was before his mother decided to leave Little Saigon, and move to San Bernadino.

"Too many Vietnamese restaurants competing in Garden Grove," she complained.

All of his friends were in Orange County, and he had begged her to stay. She told him to start packing, never mind how her half-caste son felt.

His mother harbored so many secrets. She sequestered her past like the restaurant's money she stuffed into a metal box under her bed. He remembered waking up in the middle of the night as a child to see her standing at his bedroom door in her night clothes, looking lost and terrified.

He had once overheard her talking with a customer about her first husband in Vietnam. "He was an engineer and didn't have to go and fight, but he joined Diem's army anyway, and got himself killed. He ruined my life."

Whenever he asked about his American father, his mother grew tight-lipped before muttering, "*Bụi đời.*" Dust of life. That was what half-castes like Bao were called in Vietnam. If he persisted in questioning her, she would shrug and tell him that it didn't matter anymore. They were alone now.

He searched through the chest in her bedroom for clues and discovered a cracked black-and-white photo. It pictured a young, dark-haired Mai Nguyen wearing a tight-fitting white dress and surrounded by smiling American officers. He studied their faces hoping he would recognize something of himself in one of them.

But that was in the past, as his mother often said. His future was arriving tomorrow. He finished his last cigarette and walked to the mini-mart to purchase another pack and a party-size bag of chips. On impulse, he pointed at a pint of Jack Daniel's on the shelf behind the cashier.

On the way back to his room, a young woman stopped on the sidewalk and clicked her tongue at him. She had peroxided hair and wore a scanty dress that rode halfway up her thighs. He would go out later, and check out the boulevard. Not that he would do anything. Save it for his bride.

He slipped back into his room and poured himself a drink, staring at the smudges on the blackout curtains and blowing perfect smokey rings. The sound of engines revving and gunfire blazing blared from the TV in the room next door. The headboard thumped against the wall with insistence.

He reached for the bottle again. The liquid glowed amber, reminding him of the *trà mạn sen* tea served at the restaurant. The liquor's sharp fumes prickled his nostrils.

The battering from the room next door grew louder even as the tempo accelerated. A man's groans erupted and then grew almost strangled, until they were smothered.

Bao dropped his cigarette into the glass. It hit the trace of alcohol with a satisfying sizzle, like a gasp of completion. He lay back against a pillow and fantasized about making love to Truc. He imagined how he would give himself to her. She might grow to love him, and regard him as more than just a way out of her confinement. He closed his eyes, imagining a time when they would open their own restaurant.

He woke up to shouting in the parking lot. It must be his noisy neighbors. He parted the drapes to see the young woman he had met earlier on the street. Her stark blond hair was plastered against her forehead, and her face was distorted with rage. She faced a burly, middle-aged man who wore only his underwear, and took a swing at him. "You cheating bastard!" she yelled, as she pounded him with her fists. He coupled his hands to protect his face, but tripped backwards and tumbled to the asphalt.

Bao, influenced by the alcohol he'd had, bravely took a few steps outside his door. The young woman shot him a sharp look to not interfere. It was the same expression his mother used when he asked too many questions.

The manager bolted out of the office and rushed toward the two. "What's going on here?" He pulled the woman away from her struggling victim, but she wriggled free, shouting, "Pay what you owe me, you son of a bitch!"

The man shook his head. "She's crazy." He quickly scrambled to his feet and ran into his room.

"You fucking bastard!" she shouted to his back.

The manager signaled Bao to go back inside. "I have everything under control."

He watched from the window instead.

"Leave right now, or I'll call the police," warned the manager.

The blond troublemaker crossed her arms. "Not until he pays me!"

Her client reappeared dressed, and held out several bills. "I don't want any trouble, okay?"

The manager snatched the cash from his hand. "Here's what he claims he owes you. I hope you both got what you came here for. I don't want to see either of you again."

The young woman counted the bills and jammed them into her purse before sauntering out onto the busy boulevard as if she were a beauty queen.

Bao closed the curtains, and discovered that his pint of Jack Daniels was empty.

He opened the fridge and took out the wrapped banh mi. He was happy that his mother had included her special pickled daikon.

Just the way he liked it.

PEG O' MY HEART

"I really, really hate this place," moaned Peg. Her pug nose twitched like a terrier's. "This room stinks. It's icky, and the people here are weird. I want to go home."

"We can't leave yet," explained Vicki. "We need to stay here a while longer until the sheriff can serve the restraining order."

Vicki often felt intimidated by her clever brown-haired daughter. Peg was only twelve, but she had seen through Gus right off, calling him a pot-smoking freeloader and refusing to acknowledge his existence.

Gus, Vicki discovered, was yet another sweet-talking guy who colonized the couch as soon as he moved in, the remote in one hand and a can of beer in the other. He had claimed to be temporarily out of work, but unemployment appeared to be a permanent condition with him.

At first, she didn't object to having him rooted on the couch as long as he stayed rooted in her at night. She admitted to losing all good sense when it came to sex. And with Gus, it was very good, too damn good, in fact, for her own good.

Her friend, Evelyn, had once warned her, "Love is blind, sister, but lust is deaf, dumb and blind."

Her tolerance, however, had run out one night when, after taking a bath and inserting her diaphragm—she wasn't entirely stupid—she found Gus snoring on the couch with his mouth open. Crushed beer cans and the scattered remains from a party bag of chips littered the floor. Exasperated, she shook him awake and told him that she was tired of him doing nothing. If he didn't get a job soon, he'd need to find another couch to park his ass.

He protested that he had no place else to go.

"That's your problem!" she shouted and stomped away.

He followed her into the bedroom, smiling slyly, and inserted a hand inside her shorts. When she squirmed away, he hauled off and hit her, sending her gasping onto the bed. She knew then that he would never leave peacefully.

The next morning, she left for work, and not for the first time, drove to the Wilshire Police Station to apply for a temporary restraining order. That evening, while Gus was out with his drinking buddies, she packed two bags and left the apartment with Peg. In her rush, she had left her phone behind. At least Gus didn't have her passcode.

She had tried to portray their stay at the motel as a short adventure, but Peg, after two long days of confinement, had grown restless.

"I'm totally bored being locked up in this cruddy room," she whined. "I can't even use your phone to text my friends."

"We'll return home soon, I promise. You should do your homework, and then you can watch TV."

Peg scrunched her face as if she was working out a senseless math problem. "First of all, why should I do homework when I can't even go to school? Second of all, this place only has basic cable, and there's nothing good to watch."

She was cabin crazy herself and took them to the Beverly Center. They window-shopped and had lunch before watching a romantic comedy at the cineplex. Chatting about their fun day at-large, they returned to the motel only to discover a couple screaming at one another in the parking lot.

"I really, really hate this place!" wailed her daughter. "It's your fault we're stuck here. It's because you exercise poor judgment."

At least that was what Peg once overheard her best friend's mother say. Why hadn't her own mother seen that Gus was a loser and a dirt bag? At first, he was just annoying, but then he became a total nuisance. It was the same with every guy her mother brought home. She deserved better. Vicki was so pretty with her long chestnut-colored hair and body like a pop star's. Peg sometimes wished her mother was plain. Then maybe she would meet an ordinary guy who treated her nice and had a good job so he could take them out to cool places.

"Cheer up, Peg," Her mother hugged her. "Things will get back to normal soon."

"Normal?" She broke away and rushed into the bathroom, slamming the door. Things had never been normal for them, even during those short breaks between bad boyfriends. The whole idea of having a boyfriend made her feel sick.

She gazed at her reflection in the pitted mirror. She wasn't pretty like her mother. Her hair was mousey brown, for one thing. Her hazel eyes were set much too close together, like they were trying to be cross-eyed, and she already had worry lines between her brows.

If she expected to be famous or make something of herself, she would have to rely on features other than looks. Which really wasn't so bad. What had beauty brought her mom except a worn-out couch and an empty bank account?

Her mother knocked and poked her face inside the door. "I brought my makeup kit. Why don't we take a bath together and get all dolled up?"

"Twelve-year olds don't wear makeup."

"Since when, Pegalina? You always like to play dress-up with me."

"Why bother if we'll just be cooped up in this hideous room?"

"You're no fun! It will be special, just for you and me. And afterwards, we can go to that Chinese restaurant around the corner."

Peg rolled her eyes, gazing at the spiderwebs and cracks in the ceiling. "People will think we're hookers."

"Hookers! Whatever gave you that idea?"

"All those women on the sidewalk. What else could they be?" She slipped under her mother's arm and escaped into the bedroom, staring mournfully at the dresser. She had forgotten to pack her hairbrush and her favorite pair of shorts. "I don't even have anything nice to wear."

"You can wear something of mine."

Peg pulled open the dresser drawer. It made a scraping sound as if it hadn't been used in, like, forever. She screamed and slammed it closed.

"What is it, honey?"

"I saw a humongous spider in there!" Her mother was deathly afraid of arachnids, a term Peg had learned in science class.

Her mother took a step back and knitted her brow. This made her look less pretty. It was the same expression she had whenever the toilet got plugged or when Gus left a mess in the kitchen sink. "I'm not sleeping here another night unless you kill it."

Vicki rolled up a magazine, her face now contorted in fear. Peg opened the drawer an inch and screamed at the top of her lungs. "Spiders! Hundreds of them!"

Her mother recoiled, and screamed so loud that Peg burst

out laughing.

"What's so funny, missy?"

"I was just pretending. There aren't any spiders."

Her mother swatted her lightly on the shoulder with the rolled-up magazine. "You can be so mean, you know that?"

They both burst into giggles and fell onto the bed, shrieking with laughter.

The neighbor next door pounded his fist against the wall, shouting, "Shut the fuck up!"

"Give us a break!" yelled Vicki. "Girls just wanna have fun." She leaned against Peg, and confided to her in a stage whisper. "Let's pretend that we're actually staying at a classy resort."

That would be almost impossible to do in this crummy room, but she shut her eyes anyway, and tried to picture herself sitting at a pool in a bikini and staring up at the palm trees. Someplace *really nice*, like Laguna Beach or maybe Hawaii.

But, of course, that was just dreaming. They would have to stay here until the restraining order was delivered. They would still be sleeping on this same lumpy bed tonight.

Vicki squeezed her in a tight hug and then sang in a low, lovely voice. "*Peg O' My Heart, I love you, We'll never part…*"

Peg loved her mother too, even if she did fall for crummy, stupid men.

THE RUBAB

Kyle drove Aaron to the motel and offered to get a good bottle of whiskey to share in his room, but Aaron turned his friend down. He needed to be alone to find his way out of the confusion and anger that seized him.

The motel's manager, a balding man with an oatmeal face, greeted him at the front desk. His reading glasses rested on the tip of his nose. Despite making an attempt to smile, his expression appeared permanently defeated.

"Room 11 is ready for you, Sergeant. I gave you our military discount. I appreciate your service to this country."

Aaron nodded his thanks automatically. He had grown used to hearing token praise from civilians who really had no clue what it was like.

The manager handed him the key. "How many nights will you be staying?"

"I'm not sure. Maybe a week or so. I'll let you know."

The Sunset Inn was only a few miles from his apartment and from Emily, but he might as well be back in Afghanistan.

In the early hours before dawn, Sergeant Aaron Griffin led his squad along a deserted street, separating them into two single-file lines on both sides. Rubble from a recent engagement lay everywhere. Their target, a nondescript house hidden by the neighboring buildings' rough stone walls, sat back from the street. Feeble light shined from behind its tattered curtains. One step up led to the front door.

Aaron raised his index finger, signaling Cruz and Thomas to move to the front with the push ram. Two rapid thrusts smashed the door apart, splinters flying. He barked orders, and within seconds, they were inside. Their weapon lights sent bright beams into the room's dim interior. On the left, three women in black burqas huddled on the floor, shielding a dark-haired boy and a tiny saucer-eyed girl. To the right, a bearded man in a turban squatted with unblinking eyes. His hands cradled a rifle.

"Drop it! Hands up!" These were universally recognized commands in Afghanistan. "I said—drop it!"

The man uttered what sounded like a prayer, and drew the weapon up to his chest.

A shot rang out, a breath of silence followed by a woman's screech. Aaron approached cautiously and kicked the man's calloused bare feet for signs of life. A dark stain blossomed on his victim's chest as blood seeped through his white kurta.

Aaron froze. The object he had taken for a rifle was actually a musical instrument. The bullet had passed right through its wood casing before striking the man's chest. The instrument's severed strings produced a low humming sound that still reverberated through the dark room.

The old man's eyes were open. A milky-white film covered them. The man he had taken for an assailant had been blind.

A blind musician.

As weeping from the women filled the room, Aaron kneeled before the body and attempted to stanch the wound.

"He's dead," said Corporal Hynes who stood over them.

Tears filled Aaron's eyes. The squad peered at him with startled expressions. They had never seen their sergeant show such obvious emotion, even over one of his own wounded men.

"You couldn't have known he was unarmed," Hynes reassured him.

Aaron awoke in the gloom, the motel room illuminated only by a shaft of orange light that filtered in through a gap in the curtains. He stared at a crack above the bed that began as a crevice before dividing into numerous hairline tributaries, like the mountain trails his squad had traversed in the highlands. He sat up stiffly and groaned, still queasy from all the beers he had shared with Kyle the day before.

Fucking welcome home.

During his final days in Afghanistan, he had repeated words to himself, again and again, like a mantra. "I'm going home, going home…going home…" The life that had engulfed him for the last seven years was ending. If not in infamy, then in humiliation. Brass had made an exception after his psychiatric diagnosis, and handed him an honorable discharge before completing his duty.

At the airport in Herat, he had been loaded like freight into a cargo plane along with other soldiers. In Japan, toting his duffel that held the ornate instrument wrapped in his uniform shirt, he boarded a military jet and was transported across the Pacific to Fort Irwin. After his reception stateside, a charter bus carried him past high desert towns until it plunged into greater L.A. He stared out at a city that seemed more alien to him than Kabul or Kandahar.

In San Pedro, he watched as families were reunited. Tearful wives and girlfriends hugged their returning heroes. Children folded their arms around their fathers as if they would never let go. Emily wasn't there to greet him. She had sent him a short text:

Hospital short on staff. Can't get out of work.

He boarded a service shuttle to Burbank where he ordered an Uber that took him to their apartment in Canoga Park. He felt for the loose key in his bag's side pocket and opened the front door. The furniture and framed pictures on the walls were familiar, but the place seemed as if it belonged to complete strangers.

He adopted the same hyper-alertness that seized him whenever his squad entered a house suspected of harboring insurgents. He conducted a search, investigating each room methodically. In the kitchen, the only evidence of Emily's presence was a few unwashed dishes. Her hairbrush and makeup lay on the bathroom sink. He picked up her toothbrush and placed it in the holder. His wife's casual attitude toward order often irritated the soldier in him.

Advancing into the bedroom, he passed a pile of Emily's dirty clothes. He sniffed, detecting a strange smell that wasn't hers, and scrutinized the bed closely. The comforter was pushed aside, the bottom sheet revealing only the faint impression of her body. He opened the top drawer of the dresser to discover a framed photograph buried under one of her scarves. It had been taken at their wedding. Emily, wearing a simple white dress, was tanned and glowing. He wore a blue sport coat over jeans and flashed a brilliant smile.

Aaron sat the photograph on top of the dresser where it belonged.

He returned to the living room and sank into the recliner. What the fuck was going on with her? During their last few Skypes, Emily had sounded withdrawn and evasive.

Why hadn't she made more of an effort to meet him?

To soothe his thoughts, he opened the duffel and dug under a few layers until he felt the rubab's polished surface. He pulled out the instrument carefully, almost tenderly. Its rich dark wood, decorative carving and intricate inlaid surface made the apartment seem even more lifeless. He plucked the strings before playing a simple melody the master had taught him.

Exhausted from days of travel, he soon set the rubab aside. The TV droned on as he slept, its screen emitting intermittent flashes like nighttime gunfire.

The mountain pond has frozen overnight. Children from the village gather to watch the American soldiers make fools of themselves on skates. The men's rifles are stacked against a tree. Their helmets line the shore like tiny tombstones. They joke they should be wearing them as protection on the ice. Thomas, from Minnesota, dips and twirls like an Olympic competitor. Williams, his dark face shining, his eyes gleeful, wears a bathrobe that flaps behind him as he takes to the ice. Corporal Hynes pounds the pond's surface with his skates as if loaded with gear and slogging up a mountain path. Even so, he makes fun of muscleman Cruz, accusing him of skating like an oaf. Everyone laughs.

The cold air brushes against Aaron's face as he glides across the frozen surface. He tells the kids that line the shore to join them even though the skates are too big for their feet.

Glancing behind him, he sees some of the older boys grab the rifles. They hold them up high with their arms extended like their fathers do at celebrations. He shouts at them to put the weapons down. Instead, they aim toward the pond.

Bullets ricochet across the ice. Blood spurts from Williams' head. Cruz goes down with a scream. The others hug the ground, flattening themselves against the ice as a crevice opens up and spreads quickly across the lake's surface. Rogers crawls blindly toward the gap and disappears below. Blood and splinters of ice splatter his face.

Aaron jumped up from the recliner, his foot caught in the footrest, twisting his ankle.

Emily stood just inside the door, staring at him in surprise. "Are you okay?"

He shook his foot loose and nodded. "I was having a bad dream. My squad was skating on ice…"

"How did you get in?" she asked, scrunching her eyes, as if he were an intruder who had broken into her living room.

"I had the key. I tried to reach you earlier to let you know that I was nearly home."

She breathed a weary sigh. "I had to work late, remember? How was your flight?"

"Long. The seats were hard as hell, and we basically ate field rations."

"I could make you something."

"I'm not really hungry." He rubbed the sleep from his eyes and circled his arms around her. "How are you? You must be tired, too. Maybe we should go to bed."

She shook her head and pulled away. "Aaron… I think we should sleep separately. At least for tonight anyway."

Her words were like stray bullets piercing his stomach. He swallowed hard as he grasped her shoulders. "Why do you say that?"

She avoided his eyes. "We haven't seen one another in over seven months."

"Even more reason we should—" She shook her head again.

"I'm totally beat and I need to be at work early tomorrow morning."

She turned away and retreated into the bedroom. As heat rose to his chest, he attempted to quell his anger and followed her. She handed him a pillow and a blanket, and kissed him on the cheek. Even that small sign of affection tamped down his confusion.

Re-entry was tough for both of them. It would take time. Everything would be okay. But this expectation was dashed when she quietly closed the door behind her.

That night, he lay awake on the couch, disturbed by Emily's abrupt rejection of his affection.

He woke to bright Southern California sunshine piercing through the smudged living room windows. Needing coffee, he stumbled into the kitchen where he found a note Emily had left on the counter. She had an accounting class on Tuesdays and would be home late. After pouring himself a bowl of cornflakes and downing two cups of black coffee, he put on civilian clothes for the first time in months and wandered aimlessly around the neighborhood. No one walked here. The sidewalks were merely a token nod to urban civility. The dull streets, lined with little houses that featured blank picture windows and dry grass lawns were like a bland stage set.

A loud boom from somewhere down the block made him jump, generating the same stabbing fear he had often experienced on patrol. Gang activity had increased here, he'd heard, but there were no armed checkpoints in San Fernando Valley. No hidden snipers.

He phoned Kyle.

His friend sounded stoked. "Hey, dude! I'm glad you're

back. This calls for a celebration. How about I pick you up tomorrow afternoon?"

That night, Aaron sat on the recliner with the TV on mute, strumming the rubab. He had managed to ignore the tall stack of mail piled on the floor. A few empty beer cans were scattered next to it.

Emily returned home after eleven looking tired. "How was your class?" he asked.

She pulled off her shoes. "It's tough. I always thought I was good with figures."

"I always thought you *had* a good figure." He grinned, hoping to keep things light.

She laughed. Hearing its familiar ring lifted his spirits. "You're smart. I'm sure you'll do great."

"Right now, I'm dead tired. I need to get to bed."

He leapt from the chair, maybe too eagerly. "O.K. How about I join you." He stroked her cheek and moved to kiss her neck, remembering how much she liked that. But a nightmare image came to him. A villager, a bullet through his neck, blood exploding from the wound like a red fountain.

He jerked away, and she raised her hands as if to defend herself. It was the same gesture the Afghan women made whenever his squad—large men wearing battle armor and wielding ominous weapons—appeared in their midst.

"Why did you do that, Aaron? You frightened me."

He tried to wash the memory from his head, and made light of his action. "It was nothing. Just a tic, I guess."

Her eyes told him that she didn't believe him. "I think I should—

"What's wrong, Emily? You're avoiding me."

Her expression turned suddenly fierce. "I'm avoiding *you*? That's rich, spoken by one who's always disappearing."

He recoiled from her accusation. "I've been fighting a war, Emily."

"That's been your choice, over and over. I guess you preferred quality time with your buddies in the trenches, or whatever."

"That's not how it is." He clutched her shoulder and shook it.

She pulled away from him in frank alarm. "I don't know who you are anymore, Aaron. Maybe I never did."

Fuming, he stalked away, afraid that he might hit her.

"We'll talk tomorrow, Aaron." She again closed the door behind her.

The next morning, he glumly watched Emily pull the car out of the driveway. She had claimed she was in a hurry and hadn't the time to talk. He spent the rest of his morning lodged in the lounge chair with some of the unopened mail resting on his lap. He occasionally took the rubab into his hands and strummed it slowly to settle his emotions. An instrument inlaid with shell and bone. Shells turn into bones, and bones speak.

He made a phone call to Emily at noon, but it went to voice mail. "I thought we were going to talk," he said, and hung up. They had once talked about everything, all the time. Their feelings for one another, their future, even planning to have a child.

When he shipped out for duty that first time, Emily had tearfully whispered, "Stay safe, Aaron. I want you back whole so we can spend the rest of our life together."

He had made a real effort to stay in touch during that early deployment. He phoned her often, sent texts and emails, and they Skyped whenever possible. She made him laugh, reminding him of the things that had brought them close. "Remember that seedy motel in Hollywood?" she asked. "We wondered if the cockroaches were watching us."

Emily had begged him to become a reservist and go back to college. Instead, he signed up for a second tour. He distinguished himself outside of Kabul in an operation that neutralized a group of insurgents who had attempted to infiltrate the city. He became consumed by the war. The daily fear became normal, the life-and-death threats dependable in their constancy.

On leave back home, he felt lost, as if his old life was someone else's. His friends were like strangers, and Emily seemed to grow distant. Or was it he who had grown remote?

Just before his last deployment, she accused him of desertion. "Stupid, stupid men. Always traipsing off to war. And they always come back wounded somehow."

"Look at me," he said, "I'm in one piece."

"But you're not wholly here. You left most of yourself behind over there."

He shot the blind musician two months later. It was an accident, but it tripped something new and potentially dangerous in him. He became less confident in the field, hesitating before giving orders. Self-doubt clouded him. He couldn't wipe the memory of the old man's startled expression, his bony hands clutching the instrument to his chest, the milky eyes open.

He heard that same instrument being played for the first time while leading his squad through the northern highlands. They had pushed a few ragtag mujuhedin back into the hills that day. Nighttime came fast to that part of the country. As the sun disappeared behind the high mountain peaks to the west, you could trace darkness advancing across the rugged landscape like a black curtain.

His squad was rounding a stony trail when he told his men to halt. Strains from high, wailing music were coming from the other side of a barren ridge. He didn't know what to make of it, and ordered his men to take defensive positions. He advanced toward the elevation, accompanied by Hynes and Garcia.

A village sat down below, only a few stone huts with a dozen goats enclosed behind a makeshift fence. A group of bearded men in lungis, the Afghan turban, chanted and clapped as three musicians strummed stringed instruments. The high, delicate melody almost seemed to pacify the embattled air.

Aaron shook his head, not wanting to disturb this unexpected magic, the villagers' rare joy. The spell was broken, however, when one of the celebrants pointed his rifle into the air and fired a shot that echoed against the hills.

Aaron's squad tore up the hill in response. The villagers scattered, leaving the musicians alone and bewildered, grasping their instruments protectively against their chests.

Aaron parted the curtains, dust motes scurrying in the air like a stormy blizzard, and stared out into the motel's parking lot. A man, slight and balding, was bending into the backseat of his car and lifting out what appeared to be a body. The man carried it into Room 8, returning to take out another. Aaron's teeth were set on edge. What the fuck? But after observing the situation closely, he realized that what he had mistaken for bodies were life-size dolls. He thought of his platoon, dragging away and carrying their wounded comrades out of harm's way, some to be patched up and returned to battle.

The guy has the right idea, he thought. Forget relationship drama and all the disagreements. Emily's announcement during their phone call the day before haunted him.

"I've wanted to tell you this, Aaron, but it never seemed to be the right time. I…I've been seeing someone."

He had gone stone cold, colder than he had been when seeking out the Taliban in their winter mountain hideouts.

"Who is he?"

"You wouldn't know him. He doesn't live in the Valley."

As if he couldn't possibly know anyone outside the San Fernando valley. He had only spent the last seven years on the other side of the world. He had met people, witnessed situations, she would never know.

"How long has this been going on?"

Her voice lowered to a near whisper. "I won't be coming home tonight."

"Is it him?"

"I'm staying with a girlfriend from work."

"Well, enjoy your fucking pajama party." He hung up and stormed through the apartment, slamming the walls and kicking his unopened mail furiously. He and his men had been fighting and dying so that some asshole could drive the 101 safely and fuck his wife! Rage, like an exploding IED, shook him.

His phone rang again later. He threw it against the wall.

Kyle chatted nonstop as he drove over the Hollywood Hills and through the Cahuenga Pass, his talk peppered with abuse toward the slow traffic snaking its way into the LA basin.

"I discovered this awesome bar in Sunset Junction. No pretentious aspiring models or wannabe actresses there. It's a great place to score without all the 'Oh, what-do-you-do' and 'what-kind-of–car-do-you-drive' bullshit. Not that you have to put up with any of that yourself. You've got Emily."

Aaron didn't answer, but concentrated on his breath, a technique the army psychiatrist told him would calm him when his stress level was high.

Turning off the Hollywood freeway, Kyle headed toward Sunset Junction, slowing to find a parking space. He slapped Aaron on the back as they entered the bar. Nappers featured a nautical theme that might have been sharp in the 1960s, with plastic marlin and swags of netting covering bleached plank walls. They ordered two beers at the bar before retreating to a table, where Aaron glanced out at the busy street through a porthole window. It was like looking through a rifle scope.

Kyle raised his bottle in a salute and tapped Aaron's. "So, how are you, Sergeant? It looks as if you might be home for good this time."

He was relieved that Kyle hadn't asked him why he came back early. He wasn't about to tell him about his "honorable" discharge.

"You have every right to be proud, bro."

Aaron shrugged. If his marriage was down the toilet, he could always sign on with a contractor. Black ops. But he hated those guys, making tons of money off wars without taking responsibility for their conduct.

"I can't imagine how you did it," declared Kyle. "Stay in the service for so long."

"Sometimes, I can't imagine anything else." He could have told his friend that he now realized he had been only a blip on the screen in Afghanistan. The so-called Coalition was only the latest in a long line of foreigners who had invaded the country. The instrument maker had enlightened him. Some of the rubble his squad trampled over could have been from Alexander's occupation 2500 years ago. Or the British and the Russians. The fierce, patient Afghan people had resisted and ousted them all.

Kyle held up his IPA. "A beer for your thoughts."

The war and his return home conflicted in his head. He had felt most alive in the field, where unrelenting danger dogged him everywhere. But here, in this artificial city with its indifferent people devoted to sunbathing and chasing success, they had no idea what it was like. They wanted easy myths and expected overnight victories. Shock and awe, like in a movie. Not the messy, ugly truth of war. Soldiers coming back home were like litter tossed along the side of the freeway. Once served, quickly forgotten.

Maybe Emily was right. The relationship he enjoyed with his men was more intense than the one he had with her.

"If I told you everything that I was thinking, you'd be buying until the day after tomorrow."

"In that case, I'll start by getting us another."

But instead of going to the bar, he headed for the door. Aaron caught him by the wrist. "Where are you going?"

"I need to go around the corner to get some smokes. Relax and enjoy the scenery."

The pitch-dark motel room, as dark as any black night he had spent in the Hazarajat highlands, closed in on him. He fumbled for the lamp switch, illuminating the table's pitted surface, and reached for the rubab. Fondling its familiar smooth surface, he slowly plucked its three main strings.

He had asked his interpreter what the turbaned men in the mountain village had been playing.

"It's called a rubab," said Salim, who went on to explain that it was a traditional instrument in the Middle East, "like the guitar is in the West."

Aaron had played the guitar as an adolescent, drawn to the fantasy of making loud music in front of cheering crowds, but gave it up when he realized he wasn't very good. The rubab was different. It made music like nothing he'd ever heard before. Its high, wailing strains soothed his rage and helped him to forget.

Salim must have sensed something more than mere curiosity. He told him about a street in Kabul filled with the shops of instrument makers.

"I know the very best there. Bashir is a true master. But if you visit his shop, you will need to approach him with humility and respect, not as a soldier."

He peered through the porthole window waiting for Kyle to return, imagining Sunset Boulevard as a river flowing with two opposing waves of traffic. Sleek sports cars, Benzes, Amazon trucks, and clunkers competed for space as they sped by in reasonably orderly fashion. Vehicles in Kandahar and Kabul churned unpredictably in a volatile sea of chaos. Identifying potential attackers was always a formidable challenge.

He glanced around the bar. Two guys were playing pool in the back, joking and taking their time to figure out their shots. A few afternoon drinkers sat by themselves at the bar.

The music on the jukebox changed to a low guitar wail that transitioned into a straight-ahead rock anthem, one he knew from high school days. Emily would remember it too. The last taste of beer turned bitter in his gut.

Kyle returned, smoke curling from his nostrils, and set down two beers. "Sorry it took so long. There was a hot woman on the sidewalk I needed to do an intervention with. And now I want to hear about you. How is Emily?"

"Emily is—I don't know—MIA. Things seem to have gone to shit between us."

Kyle flashed him a look of concern. "What's happening?"

He chugged down half his beer before he described the basic details of his homecoming. Emily not there to greet him, not happy to see him. "She confessed that she's seeing someone. I think she might be leaving me."

Kyle opened his mouth to say something, but then fell silent, and glanced away. After years of extracting information from tight-lipped civilians, Aaron had grown expert at knowing when people were withholding vital information.

"You've heard something about Emily, haven't you?"

Kyle hesitated. "Maybe… only through the grapevine, so it could be bullshit."

"I dealt with nothing but bullshit over there. Let me decide what is or isn't."

His friend took a swig from his bottle. "I've heard things…rumors."

"What kind of rumors."

"Supposedly, Emily has hooked up with someone from work. They've been seen together at El Nayarit. I shouldn't be saying anything, since it's just hearsay—"

Aaron put his hands up, surprising himself when he said, "I don't need to know the details, at least not this afternoon. Let's get plastered."

They avoided the subject for the remainder of the afternoon, but it rattled in his head. Emily—laughing with some guy while his squad was ambushed by insurgents. Emily—making love with some guy while he shivered in a hole seventy-five hundred miles away.

They'd had several beers when Kyle declared, "Listen, man. If you want to save your marriage, you need to kick it up with Emily."

"Kick it up? What kind of talk is that?"

"Seriously, bro. It's a fucking bad break, but it's not surprising, considering her long drought. She must have missed you."

"Yeah. Missed me so much she found herself a boyfriend."

"Listen, I'm on your side. But see it from her perspective. You've pretty much been MIA yourself. She doesn't see you for months at a time, and so she gets lonely…"

"I can't believe you're justifying it."

I'm not saying that. But with you away for so long, she's going to be jonesing for a little comfort."

"She locked me out of the bedroom, Kyle. She's my fucking wife. She treats me like I'm some stranger who's pulled a home invasion."

"Maybe she needs time to get to know you again."

Aaron thought of Emily's words on Skype from a few months ago: "You always bring the damn war home with you. It's never about us."

Kyle was talking, jamming his thoughts.

"…I'd been having trouble with Sheila and didn't know what to do about it. I was standing at the jukebox here the other day when a man came up to me…"

His friend was well meaning and generous, but lost and floating, just, he guessed, as he was.

"… and the old guy says, 'You look like you're having woman troubles. I know just what you need. Your girl will flip for this…'"

He had no idea what his next step would be. Especially without Emily…

Kyle's voice cut in again. "It turns out he was selling lingerie. He took out this sexy outfit from his case, like a magician pulling rabbits from his top hat…"

Aaron pictured the women in Afghanistan. They covered themselves from head to feet in burqas. Only their dark eyes were visible.

"I ended up blowing an entire month's drinking money on that shit, but Sheila really appreciated it. That guy was right. It worked like fucking magic."

The Beatles' "Can't Buy Me Love" was playing on the jukebox. Aaron smiled at the irony.

"I wish it was that simple with Emily."

"All I'm saying is that she must be hurting too. You need to find a way back into her heart."

Aaron spent the night on Kyle's couch. The next morning, after breakfast at a diner, Kyle drove him to his apartment and waited in the car while he threw some fresh clothes into his duffel bag. He wrapped the rubab in a towel and stowed it on top of the bag.

The light on the answering machine was blinking, but he wasn't about to risk hearing the voice of some stranger arranging a date with his wife. He started to write Emily a note. Unsure what to tell her, he fed it into the shredder.

Kyle had discouraged him from checking into a motel. "Mi sofa, tu sofa. It's yours until you sort things out."

He needed time to figure things out on his own, but it might have been a mistake to choose the Sunset Inn. Memories of the past surfaced as soon as they entered the parking court. He and Emily had lost their virginity that night when they were both eighteen.

After closing the door to his room, he detected a sudden movement to his left. He dropped the duffel and reflexively wrenched away, crouching defensively. He let out a deep breath and straightened to his full height when he realized the threat had come from his own reflection in a mirror. Buried in his thoughts of the past, he barely recognized himself now. He and Emily had undressed one another and then gazed at themselves naked together in the motel room's mirror. The nervous, skinny boy with a mild case of acne had been transformed into a tough-looking, tautly muscled product of war.

The room was as dismal as those he had stayed in on leave. Pea green walls and an archaic TV bolted to the wall. A lumpy bed that slouched toward a shabby, spotted chair. A lamp table covered with crudely engraved initials of previous inhabitants. This place had been rundown back then too, but they hadn't noticed the appointments.

He had met Emily at a club in Reseda. He might never have if it weren't for a friend shouting into his ear, "Who's that fox?" The girl stood alone, as the crowd madly thrashed around to blasting music. Her long dark hair was set against a pale complexion. She appeared way too serious in that place, where everyone was supposed to be having fun. He surprised himself by walking right up to her. He managed what must have been a lame smile and when she smiled back, he swore that it was the most perfect smile he had ever seen.

The schools they attended were miles apart, but they grew inseparable. After that astonishing night after the Prom, he knew they would get married. They had managed their work and community college schedules to spend as much time together as possible. But his enlistment had ended all that, and with each new deployment, the original outlines of their relationship shifted a bit more, until it began to disintegrate into unrecognizable fragments.

He is a drone, hovering over an indecipherable landscape. Bearded men in turbans, brandishing rifles. Women hiding explosives under their burqas. Young boys, trained as insurgents in madrasas, herding goats past a squad on maneuvers. He's on the ground suddenly, dragging a wounded man to safety behind an armored vehicle before the percussive sound of a mortar splits the dark sky again. The air buzzes with disembodied voices before they get hit once again.

He heard a loud voice outside and bolted from the bed to investigate. A grizzled man wearing a filthy overcoat was gesturing wildly and shouting, spouting the same words again and again. "Brain-drain…FBI…CIA…mind control!" A yellow mongrel joined him, barking in unison as it circled a shopping cart heaped with debris.

The manager stormed from his office. "How many times have I told you not to come into the parking court?"

The wild-eyed intruder punched the air with his fists. "You can't tell me what to do, man! You're not my brother."

The manager slumped in exasperation. "I tell you what, Jimmy. If you leave right now, I'll give you two dollars. How does that sound?"

The man, mumbling incomprehensively, offered his palm.

"You get exactly nothing until you're out on the sidewalk."

The man grabbed the cart, and with the dog following him, pushed it rattling toward the entrance.

Aaron had taken a stand a few yards away. "Sorry about all the racket," declared the manager. "Jimmy's one of those Vietnam vets. He's a damn nuisance but harmless. I sometimes offer to pay him to get lost, but he's probably already forgotten."

Returning to his room, Aaron wondered if any of his men might end up like Jimmy. Might he?

That morning, Aaron wore his uniform but left his rifle and helmet behind at the base. The shop, tacked onto the back wall of a neighborhood mosque, was little more than loose concrete blocks for walls and a tarp pulled over boards for a roof. Not exactly Walmart, as Salim had said jokingly.

He pulled back the cloth covering the doorway and ducked under its low header, halting to adjust his eyes to the shop's dim light. He gradually began to make out dozens of stringed instruments lining the walls. Others dangled from cords strung from the ceiling boards.

A small man wearing a gray turban and a spotless white salwar kameez, glanced up from his work and regarded him silently.

Aaron was on his own here without an interpreter. He knew a few phrases in Dari and Pashto, but most of them involved basic commands.

"As-Salaam-Alaikum." Peace be upon you. The customary greeting in this war-torn country.

The man approached him and bowed slightly. His high cheekbones and hawkish nose were framed by a full beard. "As-Wa-Alaikum-Salaam. Welcome. I am Bashir." Up close, the instrument maker appeared nearly as old as the blind man. His eyes, however, were extraordinarily bright and alert.

"My name is Aaron." He pointed at one of the instruments dangling in front of him. "I want to buy a rubab."

The man gazed at him like a falcon, and frowned. "I don't sell souvenirs."

He had forgotten Salim's warning about being too invasive. "I'm sorry. I didn't mean to—"

Bashir put a hand up to silence him. Despite his mocking rebuke, he untied the cord from which the instrument hung and stroked its decorated surface before motioning his guest to sit on a low wooden bench. The instrument maker took a stool facing him and propped the lower part of the rubab against his thigh. Lifting its long, sloping arm to his neck and shoulder, he placed the fingers of his left hand near the bottom of one set of strings, and those of his right at the top of the second set. Aaron noticed that, unlike a guitar, it had no fingerboard.

The melody began slowly and then rose in volume. As the tempo quickened, the tones took surprising turns, sometimes sharp and insistent, other times deep and inviting.

The music seemed to reflect the very atmosphere of Afghanistan itself. Seductive yet unpredictable, unearthly silent but capable of suddenly turning shrill and turbulent.

He thought of those joyful villagers clapping to the strange music that echoed against the stony hills. That was before the chaos. His squad hit by a mortar attack, one of his men dead. Two of the villagers shot, the rocky soil surrounding them trailed with blood. A mistaken call. The attack hadn't come from the village, but from the distant dark hills.

The instrument maker's music pulsed through him, until, with the very last chords, it carried him away from regret. Applause would have been blasphemy. Bashir's sharp eyes bore into his before he removed a particularly refined piece from the wall and placed it in Aaron's hands.

This rubab was truly a work of art, carved from a single piece of hollowed-out mulberry wood. Complex swirled carvings and shimmering inlays of shell and bone covered its surface. Bashir showed the correct way to hold it, cradled between shoulder and thigh.

He demonstrated a few chords. Aaron followed his lead, plucking tentatively. It sounded awful, like an insult, but Bashir nodded his head in encouragement. An out of step duet developed, a feeling of camaraderie. This ended abruptly when his teacher harshly declared, "No more," and snatched the rubab away.

"You don't understand." Aaron pulled bills from his pocket. "I'd like to buy it."

The instrument maker pointed to the doorway. "You should go now."

Aaron was about to protest, but remembered Salim's cautionary words. "You must approach him with humility and respect. Even so, he may throw you out just the same. He is a proud man and suffers no one."

Aaron, bewildered by the man's dismissal, stalked toward the door. As he pulled back its cloth to reveal the sun-drenched street, Bashir called out to him. "You will come back another day."

He returned to the master's shop many times, on R&R between maneuvers, even canceling a furlough to sit and learn in its dark interior. In time, he was able to play a simple melody on his own. But after each lesson, Bashir sternly removed the instrument from his hands and placed it back on its hook.

He had grown attached to this particularly remarkable instrument, but concluded that if he were to ever possess a rubab of his own, he would have to seek out another shop whose owner wasn't so damn difficult.

Not long after his summary hearing and before his final discharge papers were issued, he surrendered the instrument to his Bashir as usual, prepared to bid his teacher goodbye for the last time.

Bashir's expression remained inscrutable but then smiled for the very first time. "It is now yours." Aaron reached into his pocket, but the master shook his head. "I will not take your money."

This was completely unexpected. Overwhelmed by the

man's generosity, for the time he had spent with him and the gift he had just bestowed, Aaron thanked him profusely, bowing and setting his hand to his heart.

His teacher surprised him once again. "You should not come back."

Unsettled by the curt manner of the man, he ducked under the doorway. Holding the rubab against his chest, he marched out onto the bright, raucous street of vendors and customers for the last time.

The splendid rubab lay on the bedspread. Aaron picked it up and thought of those last moments with Bashir in his tiny shop in Kabul. It had been days later, after boarding the cargo craft in Heret, that he realized why the old master had spoken to him as if he were merely a fleeting ghost.

He had once explained that music had helped his culture survive through many centuries of foreign invasions. And like all the other occupiers before them, the soldiers of the Coalition would inevitably leave, defeated by a people it could not begin to understand. The music had brought them together only for a very short time. The gift was a farewell gesture from one of the victors to one of the vanquished.

Once again, his thoughts were interrupted by loud voices coming from the parking court. He parted the drapes to see a woman yelling at a man twice her size. "You're always expecting me to do whatever you fucking want, exactly the way you want it!"

He turned away from the window. This was none of his business. Still, he wished that Emily would scream at him like that. It might connect them, or at least bring them back to basics. She was the one person he loved most. If they were to have a future together, he needed to ask her to forgive him for his neglect. Then, perhaps, with her forgiveness, he might begin to forgive himself for the suffering and death he had signed on for all those many years ago.

He adjusted the rubab's smooth frets and began plucking the strings. A melody, high and mournful, filled the room, drowning out all the conflict, all the percussive thoughts in his head.

TOAD SCHOLARS

Edward sat staring at his glass of Scotch, lamenting his failure to square the motel's books, the numbers crooked. The accountant had come on Monday morning and barely acknowledged him before snatching the ledger from his hands and leaving in a hurry.

His brooding was interrupted by the clamor of a battered white van hurtling into the parking court. Music boomed from its bowels and reverberated against the motel's stucco walls. Screeching voices accompanied by dissonant wails and percussive thumps somehow made him imagine feeding time at the zoo. A montage of decals advertising rock groups competed for space on the van's dented sides with the name Toad Scholars scrawled in big, black Gothic script. Edward took a quick sip from his glass to bolster himself for the imminent onslaught.

The van's back door slid open with a bang. A young woman in her early twenties, flaunting spiky pink hair and a treasury's worth of ear piercings, shimmied from her seat. Her black miniskirt slid up her thighs. Edward bet she wasn't wearing anything underneath, and lowered his head to get a better perspective. She spotted his maneuver, and stuck out her pierced tongue before giving him a casual finger.

A young man, a boy with a blond buzzcut, scampered out onto the asphalt, laughing like an adolescent hyena. His midriff-baring, metallic T-shirt gleamed in the afternoon sun.

The girl swatted at him. "That's so not funny, Casey. You're such a fucking—"

"Dickhead?" someone with a deep voice in the front seat volunteered.

"More like, fag asshole!" she hissed.

Two guys clambered out from the front seats. Both wore washed-out flannel shirts, ragged jeans torn at the knees, and black Converses. Their tousled hair and unshaven stubble made them appear older than their bandmates. The driver, brown-haired, tall and lanky, sported a sparse, aspirational Vandyke. He peered at the surroundings critically. His shorter companion shook his head of curly black hair and exclaimed, "It's fucking hot here!" before stripping off his shirt to reveal a muscular torso covered with a multiverse of tattoos.

Edward recognized the cliché. The female singer with conspicuous piercings, the androgynous blond pretty boy, the lanky, good-looking lead guitarist, and the bad boy drummer. The Sunset Inn was popular with second-rate bands looking for a cheap place to stay close to the Hollywood clubs.

The blasting music persisted. Edward flung open the door and shouted, "Turn that mayhem down!" The driver lowered the stereo's volume to a level that was merely annoying.

The pink-haired girl stretched her arms to the sky, showcasing her thighs. "Amakhanian's booked us into another crap motel again!" she complained. "I can't wait to ditch these shitholes after we become famous." Clearly stoned, she nearly fell while twirling on one foot.

The driver loomed over her. "Count your fucking blessings, Shannon. We've got club bookings up the ass. Hollywood, the Valley, and Long Beach."

"I know," she said, mimicking his voice, "Quit your dreaming and scheming."

The brawny drummer glared at her. "Dream all you fucking

want, but I'm done with your scheming."

"Why, Mr. Craig," she replied in a Valley Girl's version of a Dixie Belle's accent. "*Whatever* could you *mean?*"

"You know exactly what I fucking mean, Shannon. Keep your fucking hands to yourself."

She smiled ingenuously while shooting a lascivious leer at the blond who was busy preening at his own reflection in the office window.

The drummer flexed his muscles, which made the tattoos on his chest do a dance.

"Hey you guys, knock it off!" ordered the driver. "I'm beat. Let's check in."

Sticking a cigarette between his lips and lighting it, he hustled into the office, the drummer following, and rapped his knuckles against the counter. "Yo, dude!"

"You can put that out in the ashtray in front of you," snapped Edward. "Smoking is prohibited here."

The scofflaw took a few insistent puffs before stubbing out his cigarette and strewing ash across the counter. "Our manager made reservations for us. The Toad Scholars."

Arad Amakhanian had called on the heels of the accountant's blitzkrieg. His Armenian name was right out of Glendale, but he had no discernible accent. He talked fast like one of those liability lawyers on TV, demanding two adjoining rooms for two nights. He hadn't revealed they were for a band until after his American Express Gold Card had been approved. Edward had no choice then but to book them.

He peered at his unwelcome guests. "It's all taken care of. I just need one of you to sign in."

The lanky driver had stepped over to the window, distracted by his two bandmates outside. Shannon's hands were clutching the blond boy's boney ass and pushing him against her.

"I need a signature," barked Edward.

The driver grabbed the registry and signed with his left hand. His mate signed on the line under him, a dragon tattoo stretching across his forearm.

Edward imagined how its fierce etched profile would be reduced to a wrinkled worm by the time the man was fifty. He peered at their signatures—Mitch-something-or-another, and printed below it, a single name, Cash. "You have Rooms 12 and 13, one king and two queens."

Mitch sniggered. "Two queens. That one's for Cash and the kid."

His muscled bandmate punched him in the shoulder.

Edward dropped four keys on the counter.

"Christ! No fucking card key entry?" carped Mitch, giving him a disparaging look.

"We're a traditional hostelry here." Even when irritable, he wasn't above employing irony. "You'll find a coffee-maker in your rooms, and there's a café around the corner if you want breakfast."

"I hope they're still serving breakfast in the afternoon."

"There's one more thing you need to know. The motel maintains a strict noise policy. No live music played on the property." He had been flustered by the accountant's visit and had forgotten to mention this to the band's manager.

"Man, you've got to be kidding!" huffed Cash. We've got a seriously important gig to play tomorrow night. We need to practice."

"Sorry, but those are the rules."

Mitch fumed, "Amakhanian really fucked up this time!" He stormed outside, pacing back and forth. "Hey, Arman. We're at the motel. The manager claims that we can't practice here.

What the fuck's going on? Call me asap."

"What are we going to do?" whined Shannon.

Mitch wrestled with a drum set. "I need to sleep. Let's unload the equipment." Cash picked up a guitar case and grabbed the blond by the neck, planting a kiss on his mouth before slapping him.

Edward had seen and heard enough. He retreated to his desk and shuffled through the mail. Buried among the catalogs and other assorted junk, he found an envelope addressed to him. He recognized the owner's handwriting. The man hadn't written him in years, not even a note with his monthly check. His stomach churned and the burn of Scotch prickled his throat.

The phone rang. With no introduction, the man lit into him. "I made reservations in good faith. I understand you won't allow my band to practice." Arman Amakhanian was clearly offended.

"I'm sorry. Those are house rules."

"Christ! I should have booked them at the usual place. Listen, how about we work out a deal? Maybe some extra cash for giving the band a little leeway."

Edward wasn't disposed to make things easy for him. "House rules are house rules."

"This is a major tour for the Toads. There're going to be some big music executives at the club tomorrow night. Say two big ones?"

Two hundred. Edward considered for two seconds. "How much time will they need?"

"Two hours today, maybe three tomorrow."

"Okay, but they need to keep the volume down, and I decide what that means. They need to finish by six today and they can practice from noon to three tomorrow."

"They're musicians. They don't get to bed until dawn."

"Make it two to five then." Guest check-out was at noon, and the afternoon hourlies were only concerned with their horniness. "I can accept cash only."

"I'll send it over to you by messenger," assured Amakhanian, and hung up.

Edward took a long sip from his glass. He picked up the envelope and held it in his shaking hands before slipping a letter opener around the seal and pulling out the contents. The owner's handwriting had grown unsteady since he'd last seen it, but still possessed the attributes of elegant cursive script.

Edward,

I regret to inform you that as of September the first, the Sunset Inn will be closing its doors. I began the business sixty years ago as a young newcomer to Los Angeles, but I've grown old along with the motel, which requires more improvements than is practical. My son has no interest in continuing the business. We've recently received an attractive offer from developers and have agreed to sell.

I know this leaves you out of a job, but I hope I can count on you to stay on for the next two months. Let me know your decision.

You've managed the Sunset Inn for many years now and I am grateful for your service. As a token of my appreciation, I've enclosed a check that I hope will help you make an easier transition.

Sincerely,

Samuel Avery

He let the letter fall to his desktop and peered inside the envelope. There was no check. Old Avery must have forgotten to include it. He called and left a message.

Rogelio was talking with Luisa across the parking court, her cleaning cart placed between them. He would tell him to clear out the undocumented workers living in Room 1.

But more importantly, he had to get Avery's check into his hands before the accountant reported that anything was amiss.

The Toad Scholars rehearsed loudly until eight. After the usual late-night check-ins, he finished off the bottle of Scotch and fell asleep to the drone of an old black-and-white movie featuring a detective who drank too much and had fallen in love with a gangster's gun moll.

At three a.m., he was awakened by the Toad Scholars' van returning from their gig, its stereo blaring. He opened the blinds and peered out the window.

Cash had grabbed the blond by the shoulders and was shouting, "This is what happens when you don't keep your ass where it belongs!" The boy broke away, his nose bleeding, and stomped past the office toward the Boulevard. "I hope you all go down in flames!"

Ejecting his cigarette onto the asphalt, Mitch snickered. Shannon stood off to the side in her mini-shorts, looking forlorn.

Edward slammed the blinds down, swearing under his breath. He slept fitfully, dreaming of sharing a jail cell with the bruiser, Bruno. He woke up hungover, his back muscles contracting in pain. As he stumbled to the coffee maker, he spotted the check lying on the floor beside his desk. It was made out to him for $5,000! More money than he had seen for a long time. He figured the old man must be making a bundle selling the place.

After attending to morning checkouts, he flipped the office sign to 'Closed' and rushed to the bank to cash it.

Shannon dashed into the office, pink hair a dark rose from a recent shower, her pose of smutty snark replaced with a look of distress.

"Everything has gone to fucking shit," she groaned, her lower-lip quivering.

Edward imagined she had been sent to report that the band's toilets had overflowed, no doubt after trying to flush their collection of used drug paraphernalia. Or if not that, Mitch had set the carpet on fire or Cash had put his hairy fist through a wall.

The silver stud under the girl's lower lip glinted as she turned chatty. "Mitch and Cash decided to go out to score a little something before the gig last night, and when they returned, they caught me in bed with Brian. Mitch thought it was funny. He said that I was moaning louder than he'd ever heard me on stage. But Cash was all bent out of shape. He went into a rage, and said that if one of us didn't go he'd dissolve the band."

Why is she telling *me* this? thought. Edward. I manage the motel, not the band.

Shannon ran a hand through her pink hair. "Cash is such a jealous bitch," she spat. "We had an important gig to play last night, but he said that he didn't give a fuck. Mitch managed to talk him down, but Cash was royally pissed all night. You should have heard our audience whoop and cheer when he slapped Brian during our second set."

"We really slammed that last set, but you wouldn't know it from the bad vibes in the van later. Cash and Mitch decided that it was Brian who should go, and now he's left. I told them we had to find him. He isn't the greatest guitarist, but our audiences love him. He has this incredibly sexy, androgynous appeal. So now we're going out to look for him."

Relationships were way too complex these days, thought

Edward. Much too complicated for him, at least.

The band's van pulled to a stop in front of the office, the speakers booming, Mitch motioning Shannon to join them. "I think we lost the keys," she shouted, as she ran out the door.

The Toad Scholar's decal-adorned rattletrap roared away, a cloud of acrid exhaust trailing behind it.

Edward glanced at Avery's letter sitting on his desk, and wondered what belongings were worth taking with him when he left his job. That is, if he wasn't destined to suffer a cellmate named Bruno.

VISITATION RIGHTS

Darrisha had washed and styled her hair that morning before packing her makeup, a photograph and the new shoes and floral dress into a small vinyl suitcase. At the end of her shift, one of the counselors jokingly asked if she was planning to run away.

"I'm not running nowhere. I'm *going* somewhere. I'll see you all tomorrow."

On Sunset, she spotted a cab and raised her free arm. As it pulled to the curb, a young white woman with a diaper bag hanging over her shoulder and carrying an infant flung the back door open and scooted in.

"Damn! That was my ride!" Darrisha's voice dribbled into exasperated silence as the cab sped away. It was rush hour, and there were few cabs in LA to begin with. She walked to the bus stop and waited a full half hour until, blowing exhaust behind it, the 66 lumbered to a stop.

The Sunset Inn would give her privacy and it was close to the restaurant. She had called the motel's office two days ago and told the manager she wanted to reserve a room, but she didn't have a credit card to hold it. He promised to hold one for her until 5pm. Losing that cab was going to make her late.

She rushed into the office, out of breath, and found the manager bent over his desk. "Hello? I'm Darrisha Williams. I called about a room. I hope it's still available."

The man came up to the counter and met her eyes, his sour expression transformed into a welcoming smile. "No problem, miss. I'm holding Room 14 for you. Queen bed, non-smoking. It's eighty dollars with tax."

She counted out four twenties, proud to spend the money from her first paycheck, especially for something she had been wanting for a very long time.

The manager peered at her intently and handed her the key. "Have a good stay. I'm Edward. If there's anything you need, please let me know."

As she walked to her room, she passed curtains parted to reveal a young woman's pale face, her eyes blinking against the late afternoon light. She was the thief who had stolen her cab. She was sure she had seen her at the clinic.

Locking the door behind her, she leaned against it with a sigh of relief. The room wasn't much to look at, but after being forced to share a space with others for so many years, it seemed like a palace.

She took out the framed photograph from her bag and placed it on the chest. It had been taken of Janay three years ago. She was turning thirteen. It was her birthday and they were getting together tonight.

Her daughter's first visit to state prison must have been awfully scary. The ID inspection, the search, the clanging gates, the long echoing hallway filled with the strange belligerent noise of prison life. The visiting room with its worn plastic chairs bolted to the floor and the tables set too close for any real privacy, was devoid of any welcoming element.

Darrisha would never forget the clicking sound of Janay's beaded braids when her eight-year-old girl entered the room. It had been like music. But the look of fear in her daughter's face was heartbreaking. Her eyes darted about in bewilderment, glancing everywhere except at her mother. The child she had last seen had grown into a nervous, gangly girl, but she instantly recognized her. The same warm brown complexion, stick-limbed coltish slightness, and dark eyes observing everything as if meant only for her.

Janay sat at the table directly across from her. The woman from Child Services softly informed, "This is your mother."

Darrisha swallowed, ashamed that she should need an introduction, as if they were strangers meeting for the very first time. More than anything, she wanted to hug her little girl, but Janay crossed her arms and refused to acknowledge her. Darrisha felt a pain in her chest, like her heart was being stabbed.

"I'm so happy to see you, Janay. You've grown so much." Her daughter stared blankly, as if the person sitting across from her was just another one of life's unwelcome surprises.

Darrisha tried to hide her disappointment. She wanted to apologize for leaving her baby alone for so long. She wanted to tell her that she would make it up to her someday. Instead, she resorted to small talk, as if the bad had never happened. As she continued to chatter away, the girl looked right through her before adopting a mask of boredom. It seemed an eternity before the guard announced that visiting hours were over. As the woman from social services took her daughter away, she tried to grasp her hands. She returned to her block, cursing and angry at herself, kicking her cell's door after it clanged shut and stifling her sobs so that her hard-ass cellmate wouldn't hear.

Janay was eleven when she visited again. Darrisha was told that she had been shuttled from one foster home to another, from one social worker to the next. Her daughter appeared more composed, no longer the fearful fledgling. She understood that her mother had done some bad things, and peered at her with undisguised defiance.

Darrisha's questions about her school and friends elicited only a shrug. She hoped to break her daughter's sullen silence by telling her that she had decorated her "room" with photos taken of Janay, along some of her drawings that child services had sent. Meeting silence, she could hear her voice pitching higher in futile optimism as she described her role in "For Colored Girls Who Have Considered Suicide" performed at the prison. Janay furrowed her forehead in bland disinterest.

She achieved a breakthrough, however, when she asked her daughter what kind of music she liked. The girl seemed to consider this, and then replied, "I like Demi Lovato and Elle Varner, but I like Beyoncé more."

Darrisha told her that Beyoncé was popular with the inmates too. They even held look-alike contests, pooling their cosmetics and hair extensions, and lip-synching to CDs on a boom box in the common room. Her daughter's lips curled in a cautious smile.

Just before visiting hours ended, Darrisha placed the necklace she had made in workshop into the girl's hands. A chain of colorful beads that matched the ones Janay had worn in her braids on the first visit. A guard strode toward them, prepared to investigate the exchange, but the woman from social services indicated that it was okay.

It was pitiful, really, but it was the only thing she had to give her daughter. Janay peered at her gift critically, but then— a small victory—she fastened it around her neck.

Darrisha spread the floral cotton dress on the bed, stroking it smooth before she stepped into the bathroom. It was a luxury not to have someone always waiting behind her to use the sink.

She examined her face in the mirror. Prison hadn't entirely robbed her of her looks. Her complexion was clear, and except for a few strands of grey, her hair was still dark and thick.

She touched the scar on her cheek, a relic from the last time Press had beaten her. That was just before they were arrested for selling crack to that rich asshole attorney from Sherman Oaks. Press had stayed in the car, claiming he needed to keep watch, and sent her to close the deal. The judge handed him two years. With a previous conviction, she was given six for possession and dealing. The white attorney got off with a reprimand and twenty hours of community service.

Four years ago, after he was released, Press visited her. "You got a prison face," he said, curling his lips in a shit-eating grin.

"What does that mean?" she asked, playing his game.

"Like a tattoo. Somethin' hard to get rid of."

She told him not to bother visiting her again. No way she was going to deal drugs from the inside. "I want out of here, not a life sentence."

It had been tough keeping a low profile all that time, when everyone played with her head or pushed her ass around. But she kept her head down, working every day in the laundry before she got assigned to the library. She learned to use the computer, and spent most of her off-time reading in her cell. What interested her most were the books about addiction—the story of her life. She saw the prison counselor on a regular basis, a young white woman who recommended early release. The parole board denied her the first time, citing her multiple counts. It went better the second time.

It had been months now since her release, but she still didn't feel free. She had been required to register as a drug offender, and was placed in the conditional release program at Open Doors Reentry Center.

Her parole officer, Layne, a lesbian who revealed that she and her partner cared for two foster kids, kept her parolees on a short leash. The woman talked tough, but still encouraged her. "I believe in you, girl. You just might make it."

She found employment at Open Doors' rehab clinic off Sunset, where a few former addicts assisted the counselors. It was strange doing data entry about the clinic's clients, details that eerily matched her own past life.

At first, whenever she asked permission to see Janay, Layne would shake her head, and say: "Give yourself a while longer."

With only one goal in mind, she proved that she was responsible. She was even asked to conduct an AA meeting at the Center.

She was finally allowed visitation rights. "But only under supervision," explained Layne.

"I don't want to meet her like I'm still some goddamned prisoner."

The woman chuckled. "You may no be longer incarcerated, but there are rules attached to your parole."

Darrisha pleaded to see her daughter alone. After several consultations among the Center's counselors, she was granted her request. But her appeal to spend a night away from the Center was denied.

"What? You think I'm a flight risk or something?" she asked Layne, who arched her shaggy eyebrows.

"We're just protecting you from becoming one."

Mrs. Bridges, Janay's current foster parent, was uncooperative on the phone.

"I have a right to see her!" Darrisha insisted. "The law says so. I'll make a complaint." The woman received six hundred dollars a month from the state for fostering. A complaint might bring out an investigator.

Mrs. Bridges grudgingly agreed.

"Is Janay a good girl?" She knew so little about her daughter.

"She's well-behaved, but awfully quiet," replied Mrs. Bridges in a clipped voice. But you never know, boys or gangs..."

"I hope she isn't getting into any trouble."

"No more than any girl who doesn't have responsible parents to look after her."

Darrisha ignored the comment. "Does she ever talk about me?"

"Never," said Mrs. Bridges, with spiteful finality.

She told the woman that she would phone after school. When Mrs. Bridges claimed that her daughter didn't want to talk with her, she barked, "I'll just keep calling until she does."

That afternoon, Mrs. Bridges answered once again, and, letting out a weary sigh, called, "It's for you Janay." Her daughter breathed a wary hello, and then fell silent.

"I think about you all the time," breathed Darrisha. "I'm going to see you soon."

Her baby answered by hanging up.

She broke into tears that evening during her reentry group meeting. They encouraged her to keep on trying.

With every call, Darrisha talked into the silence until one day, she announced, "I want to celebrate your birthday with you." Janay's reply, soft and high, was like a long-awaited song release. "I guess we could see each other."

She again pushed her counselors to spend the night on her

own. "I want to be free to take my birthday girl to dinner, not feel like some tagged ex-con."

A few days later, Layne called her into her office. "They've agreed to give you a benefit of a doubt." Pointing a warning finger, she gave notice. "But you must report to Open Doors the next morning by 8am before you go into work."

She closed the plastic curtain and stood under the shower, humming to "I'll See You Soon," a song the inmates had played in the Day Room for a long time.

She was going to see her baby. They were meeting at La Fiesta for an early dinner. Mrs. Bridges had agreed to drop Janay off at the restaurant. She would pick her up before nightfall.

Wearing her new dress, she walked into the motel office and asked the manager if she could use the phone to call a cab. He told her that he'd call a reliable service for her. While she waited for her ride, he introduced himself as Edward.

"Are you going someplace special, dressed up so nice like that?"

"It's my daughter's birthday. I haven't seen her for a long time."

A wistful look came over his face. "I have a daughter too. I hope to see her one day."

At La Fiesta, she took a front table and ordered a margarita. She would have just one. The restaurant matched its name. The waiters wore colorful vests and shiny sombreros, swinging from table to table to Mariachi music that was like a merry-go-round of sound. It was a perfect place to celebrate her daughter's birthday.

Still, she glanced around with uncertainty, nervous about spending unstructured time alone with her girl. It might end up like those terrible meetings in the prison's visiting room.

An hour later, sipping her drink and telling the waiter she was waiting to order, she realized that Janay wasn't showing up.

She called twice from the restaurant's pay phone, but there was no answer. After the second attempt, she marched back to her table, slapped down a twenty to pay for the basket of chips and her half-finished drink, and blindly rushed out the front door. She raced into the street, and lost a shoe halfway across. As she bent down to grab it, the wind draft from an oversized pick-up truck nearly knocked her over. Cars honked as she limped to the curb and flopped down on a thin wedge of sparse, littered grass.

A man threw a beer can from a passing car, shouting, "Hey, baby! You want to fuck?"

Their special evening together was broken, like the heel on her shoe. *I bet that Bridges bitch didn't even tell Janay where we were supposed to meet.* The familiar feeling of rank despair took her, the weight of powerlessness that always made her want to get high.

A young couple wearing tank tops and cutoffs displaying a riot of tattoos, tripped by. She bet they knew where to score. *I can't screw up now or I'll never get Janay back.*

She stood from the curb and shook the dry grass and debris from her dress. The world seemed to suddenly spin around her, and she stumbled.

A skinny young white man with blond dreadlocks startled her, snorting and grinning like a corrupt preacher. "Where you staying, baby? I'll take you home."

She pushed him away and hobbled along the sidewalk. He trailed her, shouting,

"Wait up, baby. "You wanna get high with me?"

She passed the darkened window of a storefront and caught

her reflection. Her carefully-forked hair now stood out in uneven patches, her mascara had run from tears, bruising her eyes.

The motel's neon sign blinked uncertainly a block away. Her stalker was right behind her.

She swung her bag at him. "Get the fuck away!"

He caught her arm. "You don't mean that, now. I only want to brighten your night."

Shaking from his grip, she fled toward the entrance. Light from a TV in the motel's office flickered through the windows, seeming to make the flower prints on her dress agitate. As she dug for the key in her bag, the man was on her. She screamed and struggled against him, pounding her fists into his chest.

All the men who had used and abused her. The waste of all those years incarcerated. This night's disappointment.

Enraged, she swiped the end of the key across her attacker's face. He brought a hand to his cheek and peered at the blood on his palm in disbelief. "I'll kill you, bitch!"

The manager ran out of the office. "Hey! What's going on here?"

"None of your business!" hissed Dreadlocks.

"Everything here is my business!" shouted the manager, revealing a baseball bat from behind his back and brandishing it. "Now get the hell out of here!"

The man pointed a finger at her, snarling, "I'll see you later!" and retreated toward the street, his curses dissolved by gunning engines and blasting stereos out on the Boulevard.

Shaking and gasping for breath, she leaned against the wall to steady herself.

"Are you okay?" asked the manger, dropping the bat on the asphalt and approaching her.

She nodded. "I think so. Thank you for coming out."

"It's my job. I don't like to see my guests being threatened. Was that guy a boyfriend or something?"

"No. He was bothering me on the street."

"You best stay in your room for the rest of the night. That's a safer place to be than on the streets. Remember, call me if you run into any trouble."

"I was supposed to meet my daughter tonight," she confessed.

He snapped his fingers. "I almost forgot. There was a phone call for you. I believe I took the message down right." He escorted her across the parking court into the office. She was still shaking. He offered her a chair and removed a tack from a folded piece of paper on the corkboard and handed it to her.

She opened it with trembling hands.

Janay called. She couldn't get a ride and is sorry she couldn't meet you. Please call her tomorrow after school.

Tears flooded her eyes.

"Is everything okay?" The manager hesitated before putting a hand on her shoulder.

"I wanted to see her so bad tonight."

"It sounds like you will, just not tonight. Let me walk you to your door. That bastard might make good on his threats and come back."

Inside her room, she shook off her ruined dress and stood under the shower for an eternity, washing away the rank smell of her attacker, the assaulting force of his filthy hands. She always believed that she was strong, but maybe Layne was right. She wasn't prepared for the realities on the outside.

Later, crouched on the bed, Darrisha rocked, pretending that her baby girl was in her arms. And then, before falling asleep, she prayed for the first time since she was a stray, feral child with her grandmother in Louisiana.

She stopped at the office the next morning. The manager—Edward, she remembered his name—was dressed in a light blue sport shirt and pressed dress pants. He had shaved and combed his hair, what there was left of it, in sparse neat rows.

"You look nice," she said. "Is this a special day?"

"You could say that." He looked at her with the same pointed interest he had shown when she first checked in. "How about a cup of coffee? I brought donuts from around the corner."

Was this man flirting? She sat on a stool near the coffeemaker. "How long have you worked here?"

"Way too long. And what about you?"

She was not used to a stranger asking about her life. "I work at Open Doors. I'm not a counselor, just a client they gave a job to."

"I heard about that place. There was a story about it on the news."

"Thank you again for your help. I don't know what would have happened if…"

"Believe me, it's all in a day's work. The boulevard attracts all types."

She set her coffee cup down. "I guess I should get to work myself."

A smile lingered on his face. "I'm calling a cab. I don't want you getting into any trouble with that druggie again."

He offered his hand to shake. "I hope you have a great time with your daughter. Maybe I'll get to meet her someday."

Without thinking, she pecked him on the cheek. And then, just before leaving, she double-checked to make sure Janay's message was still safe in her pocket, proof that her baby wanted to see her mother.

HIDEAWAY LOUNGE

Bernie was intent on leaving a paper trail, and offered the credit card he often gave his son to use. The manager seemed to peer at him curiously, as if wondering why an elderly gentleman with a respectable local address would be checking into the motel. How was the man to know what he and Margaret had planned?

Piebald on top, with white hair hanging in long wisps on the sides and at the back, Bernie Lauer resembled a retired symphony conductor or perhaps a celebrated novelist. Despite his frail appearance, one could tell that he had once been a substantial man.

The oncologist advised withdrawing chemotherapy for his wife. Margaret's treatment was proving ineffective, and was compromising her quality of life. The doctor had used the phrase, "during the remaining time left for her."

Bernie had spotted an article about the Sunset Inn in the LA Times. *The motel was described as "a crumbling relic from Hollywood's heydays." It was being slated for demolition to make way for yet another mini-mall. The story and accompanying photos included a profile on a writer who was staying there to gather material for his next novel before its imminent destruction.*

He read the story to Margaret out loud, and her face brightened. "Our honeymoon motel is getting some well-deserved attention in its sunset years." Her voice was weak, but spirited and still beautiful to him. Her hair had turned white long ago, absent in patches now from the drugs, but her face seemed as luminous as it had been on that very first day they met.

She grabbed his hand, and whispered, "I have something important to ask you. Please listen to what I have to say."

Bernie was twenty-four when he had arrived at LA's Union Station. It was 1956. He carried a battered leather suitcase that held a single suit and a pencil-marked screenplay he had labored on over the last year. He had arranged to share a rental with his college friend, Warren. It was a two-bedroom on Beachwood, only a few blocks from renowned Hollywood Boulevard, a world away from his single room on the southside of Milwaukee.

Everything here appeared exotic to him. The busy freeways, the landmark mountains and dusty palm trees, the sun-struck streets where no one need wear an overcoat to ward off the cold. The city seemed to stretch on forever, as uncontained as his ambitions.

The taxi let him off on a quiet block in front of a faux-French Neoclassical stucco building, complete with turrets at the corners and a deep, shingled mansard roof. He walked into a courtyard that featured a gurgling fountain and impossibly thick bushes rife with colorful flowers, which he later learned were fuchsias and bougainvillea. Warren welcomed him with a hug and offered him a drink before leading him to a small patio where they gazed up at the Hollywood Hills talking about old times and the future. His bedroom was tiny but he could open the French windows wide to take in the hazy hills and fragrant scents. He was convinced that he had found paradise.

But he needed to find work. He had two local theater productions of his plays under his belt back home. Not much, but it was something. They were variations on Thornton Wilder's plays, working-class stories that reflected the culture of his native city, with its labor unions and socialist mayor. The critic at the *Milwaukee Journal* had praised his first play for "its convincing truths and strong characterizations that underscore the everyday struggles of the working man." Bernie had turned his second effort into a screenplay. Not exactly Hollywood material, but the writing might justify being hired by a studio.

Warren, on contract with Warner Brother's Pictures, introduced him to a friend of a friend of the assistant to a vice president at Universal-International Pictures. The assistant placed Bernie's screenplay into the inbox of the VP, who despite the distraction of drinks and dames, managed to read it over a weekend in Palm Springs.

Warren reported Monday's office conversation to Bernie, all thirdhand.

"Who's this Bernie Lauer guy, anyway?" asked the VP, plopping the manuscript on his assistant's desk.

"He's some new kid from Milwaukee," she said. "He wrote a couple of plays that got decent reviews. I thought you might want to take a look. I hope I didn't make a mistake."

"The script itself will never sell. It's much too political. But his plotting is damn good, and most of the dialogue is strong. The boy's got talent. Let's bring him in and see what he can do."

Bernie couldn't believe his good fortune. He was dazed for those first weeks sitting at a table on the Universal lot and tossing around story concepts with a half dozen other "hacks for hire," as the cynical writers called themselves. The project they were assigned to was based on a controversial novel. It would require much watering down if the studio were to throw any money into it. Rumors galore already surrounded it. Lana

Turner, currently in the midst of a fifth divorce and supposedly dating a gangster, was interested in playing the female lead. If she accepted the role, the studio chiefs would certainly green-light the film. It was pretty heady stuff for a boy from the Midwest.

Bernie often met Warren at the Hideaway Lounge after work at their respective studios. The bar, a small place located at the Sunset Inn on Hollywood, attracted not-so-famous industry types: writers, camera men, set technicians, makeup artists. To enter the dimly lit room from the bright Southern California glare reminded Bernie of visiting a movie house for an afternoon matinee. It always took him a while to accommodate himself to its darkness.

The Hideaway featured a half-pint bar presided by a crackerjack bartender. Its cozy nightclub atmosphere was enhanced by tiny round tables and the shaded lamps were perfect for exchanging industry gossip. A smart black leather banquette along the back wall encouraged canoodling.

"You can get a room here if you run across a willing broad," Warren frequently repeated, often pointing to a lothario leaning against the bar talking up a bleach blonde wearing too much makeup.

Bernie couldn't quite picture himself picking up a girl and checking into a room. Well, he *could* imagine it, but…

Maybe around his sixth visit, he opened the Hideaway's door with Warren behind him, and spotted her. She held a drink and was laughing at something the bartender had just said. The ceiling fan ruffled her chestnut hair, raising energetic little wisps around possibly the most beautiful face he'd ever seen. She was twenty-three, twenty-four at most, he guessed, but her clear, deep-throated laughter cast her as older.

He quickly strode up to the bar before the spot next to her

might be taken.

Warren called to him. "Hey! Wait up, buddy!"

Bernie stood right next to her and smiled tentatively, prepared to be rebuffed.

The woman stood her ground—with no shy deflection—and smiled back at him.

"So, what'll you gentlemen have?" asked Clarence. Unlike many, he was a skilled professional, not some aspiring actor who played bartender before his big break.

"Dewar's on the rocks," ordered Warren.

Milwaukee had mostly been a beer town, but Bernie had already learned that ordering a Schlitz didn't mix well in Hollywood. He pointed at the woman's amber-colored concoction. "I'll have what she's having."

Warren, seeing his friend on the make, shot him a glance of approval.

Bernie met the woman's eyes. Brown. Filled with playful amusement. As far as he could tell, she wasn't wearing any makeup. She didn't need to.

"What *are* you drinking anyway, if I may ask?"

"Yes, you may. It's a Manhattan. Would you like a taste before you order?"

She offered her glass.

Warren coughed, and nudged him with his elbow.

His fingertips brushed hers as he took the glass. The drink was a bit sweet but it went down warm and smooth in his throat. Handing it back to her, their fingertips met once again, warm against the cold glass.

A more serious expression replaced her look of amusement. "Do you like it?"

He motioned to the bartender. "I'll take Manhattan." She didn't laugh at his bad joke, but at least she didn't groan.

"Excuse my manners. I'm Bernie."

She offered her hand. "I'm Margaret. It's nice to meet you."

It looked like a handshake, but it felt like something else.

"Would you like another?" he asked.

"Oh, no thanks." She laughed. "One's more than enough for me. I'm happy that you helped me out with this one."

"I've never forgotten the good times we had there," whispered Margaret. "That tiny lounge, so dark and intimate. It always seemed a surprise when we entered it from the bright street."

His gnarled hand grasped her shoulder. "You were always my surprise."

She pushed herself up against the headboard, a brief flicker of unexpected energy.

"You were so shy, straight from the Midwest. And broke too. You wore a wool suit in the summer."

"It was my only suit."

She attempted a laugh but gasped for air instead.

"What can I do?" he appealed. "I want to help you, but I feel so helpless."

She took several deep breaths. "I know you do, dear, but I'm tired of needing help. It'll only be a short while, anyway, won't it?"

The Hideaway was packed by six pm. Animated conversation and laughter had risen to a high pitch, but Bernie barely noticed.

Margaret still nursed her drink. "Do you work at one of the studios?"

He was already on his second. "I just started at Universal."

"You're a writer." It wasn't a question.

"How did you know?"

"You look like a writer."

"You mean, I'm not some handsome, well-dressed leading man?"

Margaret blushed. "I mean, you look smart and sensitive."

"Sensitive, maybe. Smart, I'm not so sure."

"What are you working on?" She seemed to be genuinely interested.

"It's only speculative at this point. I sit in an air-conditioned room with other simians. We toss around various ideas until we come up with a banana ripe enough for our boss to consider worth peeling."

She laughed. "So, I guess *you're* the one who comes up with the bad metaphors."

"You could say that."

Their conversation came easy. Bernie waved to Warren and they slid past the tables to the banquette in the corner. He wanted to know more about Margaret. Or maybe just be with her, to swim in the wake of her voice.

She told him that she was an assistant to the president of one of the film unions. "The cameramen, wardrobe mistresses, and carpenters make entertainment in America possible," she said, "just like autoworkers make it possible for Americans to drive. It's tough going now, though, with the anti-communist crusade so strong. Some people are calling us commies."

"This isn't some kind of elaborate recruitment effort, is it?" he asked.

She gave him a sly look. "And what if it is?"

"I'd join your union in a heartbeat. Where do I sign up?"

Her laughter rose above the buzz of the cocktail-hour crowd. "I'm afraid that we don't represent writers."

"That's too bad. Maybe I should change jobs."

"Oh yeah? Would that be easy for you?"

"Sure. I'm a pink diaper baby. My dad's a socialist union man and a big supporter of our so-called Commie mayor back in Milwaukee. I voted for him just before I blew town."

"A man after my own heart."

She was unbelievable, this Margaret. She didn't wait for social cues, but initiated them, as if she understood his need to be led a little—away from his desk and his typewriter and his made-up stories.

A photographer approached them carrying an Agifold camera with an oversized flash as she made her rounds. "Margaret Wells. I haven't seen you for a while."

"Hi, Sally. I want you to meet Bernie Lauer. He's a writer at Universal."

"More like a scribbler than writer," he demurred.

She put her hand on his arm. "Don't you believe it. He's one of the best."

"I should hire you as my agent."

Sally raised her camera. "So, what are you working on?"

"Nothing special." The studio had sworn them all to secrecy and would have his head if he let the cat out of the bag.

"Nothing Special? Gee, interesting title. I can't wait to see it."

The flashbulb flashed. The cold, bright light bounced around the darkened room like quicksilver

The photo appeared on page five of *The Hollywood Reporter* the next morning. The headline: "Union on the Boulevard." Margaret was smiling into the camera, holding her drink up in a toast. Bernie was identified as "Hollywood's hottest new screenwriter." He looked serious, even a bit irritated by the invasion of privacy.

Margaret made her case rationally. Her matter-of-fact resolve shocked Bernie. He told her that he wouldn't even consider it. They held hands in silence until she fell asleep.

But she continued to press him for days.

He broke down one evening, sobbing, He said that he might agree, but with one stipulation. "I want to do this with you. It's the only way I will help you."

She was horrified. "No, Bernie. You won't! It's me who's dying,"

"You're everything to me. Life without you is no life at all."

"You can't be serious."

"I won't help you if you don't agree." They discussed it every day.

She would shoot him a look mixed of contrition and appeal. "Are you sure you want to go through with this?" she asked again and again. "I wouldn't blame you if…."

"I've never been more certain of anything since the day I asked you to marry me."

She managed to muster a smile. The pain was much worse, he knew, more than she ever showed him.

He stroked her pale forehead. "We've discussed this from every angle. It's what I want too."

Bernie considered that first meeting with Margaret as the true beginning of his life in California. On their fifth date, he worked up the courage and asked if she would like to spend the night with him.

She kissed him. "I thought you'd never ask."

"My place isn't exactly set up for entertaining. Would you mind if I got a room?"

He hightailed it to the office, paid for the night, and picked up the key for the sole vacancy. Room 16. They left the Hideaway separately, for discretion's sake, as if the other patrons weren't already winking. He was a virgin, but pretended he was merely inexperienced. She led him through a ritual of stroking, kissing, caressing, and passionate love-making. He felt doubly lucky because his first time was with someone he loved.

They became regulars, asking for Room 16 all during their courtship.

Warren half-jokingly suggested they choose the Hideaway Lounge for their wedding reception. "You'll find most of the guests drinking at the bar after the ceremony anyway."

Bernie shook his head. "It's too small, I'm afraid. I think Margaret is inviting the entire union." His guest list was limited to a few writers he knew from the studio and a scattering of acquaintances he'd made since arriving in LA. He promised his parents that he would bring Margaret to Milwaukee soon.

The wedding took place at the Roosevelt Hotel. As Warren predicted, more than a few guests broke for the Hideaway afterwards for a nightcap or two.

The couple settled into a small apartment on Ivar. It boasted a sunny patio and had a walk-in closet that accommodated a desk for him.

One Monday morning, Bernie came into the writer's room and saw two vacant chairs that had been occupied by guys he had traded script ideas with on Friday. "Where are Max and Joseph?" he asked.

The head writer looked up from his papers. "Their loyalty to our project was called into question. They were fired," His explanation sounded false, rehearsed.

Bernie complained to Margaret over dinner out that night. "I came to Los Angeles to escape Midwest provincialism. Now we're all being handcuffed by these hysterical Commie hunters."

She grimaced. "When that traitor Reagan was president of the Screen Actors Guild, he caved to the fascists and became Senator McCarthy's quisling. We've lost so many good people to the blacklist since that time, certainly some of the most principled."

Someone must have overheard her, and not long after that, Margaret was, absurdly, subpoenaed by the House on Un-American Activities Committee.

"The witch hunters must be getting desperate," she declared. "I'm just a glorified union secretary."

The Committee had lost its teeth by then and she was never called to testify. But a subpoena was enough to make people— even some friends— distance themselves from her, and by association, from Bernie. Warren's sudden absence especially hurt him. There were also shifts happening at the studio. His reputation there had risen among the ranks of writers, but then it seemed to sink. Was this about his talent? Or was it studio and national politics?

Despite the atmosphere of uncertainty surrounding them, they pooled their resources and bought a modest house in the Larchmont district, only a dozen blocks from two major studios. Bernie walked to work so Margaret could commandeer the Chevy Bel Air for her union rounds.

Imitation of Life finished production and was released in 1959. Despite the double scandals of a fifth divorce and her reported relationship with a gangster, Lana Turner had starred in it. The film received good reviews, but its controversial take on class and race relations was too radical to be considered for an Oscar. Bernie's name didn't appear anywhere in the credits, but he was proud of his contribution to his first major project. With the small bonus he had received, he and Margaret flew to

Europe.

In Paris, they discovered a tiny bar in Montparnasse that reminded them of the Hideaway Lounge, which, to their astonishment, made them feel homesick. On the way back, they took the train from Chicago to Milwaukee so that Margaret could finally meet his parents. Unsurprisingly, the smart young woman with Leftist credentials was a big hit. Bernie actually felt a bit jealous over the way his parents doted on her.

Back in Hollywood, his fear that his work with Universal might be ending was confirmed when he was pulled from script development and consigned to editing the work of other writers, most of which he found half-baked and pedestrian.

"It's time we have a child," announced Margaret,

Emily arrived ten months later.

One night, the baby asleep in her crib, Bernie sat with Margaret at the kitchen table. He was drinking Scotch and feeling morose. "The studio has condemned me to plugging holes in Swiss cheese."

She took his hand. "I know it may be small comfort to you, but you still have a good-paying job, as thankless as that may seem at times. You have Emily too, and—"

"I have you. I'll never forget that."

"I'm worried about Emily and Aaron," said Margaret. "Do you think our letter will help them understand our decision? Will they ever be able to forgive us?"

She pushed herself up from the bed with a groan. "We do worry, don't we? How terrible it will be for them."

Their decision would seem inexplicable, and terrible. They had tried to make it easier with the short letter they were writing, expressing love for Aaron and Emily, and assuring them that they were fully aware of what they were doing. All the practical and legal matters had been taken care of.

"You know," she whispered, "you can still carry on without me."

He kissed her forehead. "No. I couldn't."

Bernie was dropped from Universal. It was a change he almost welcomed. He soon found a place at MGM. Margaret, up to her ears in diapers and doctor appointments for Emily, missed working with the union. He felt guilty about this. He hadn't focused on her needs, consumed by how his talent had been squandered at Universal.

His discontent had caused him to wander. He often claimed he had to work late when in fact he spent those evenings with a young female writer at her apartment in Los Feliz. That relationship lasted for only a few months, but he continued staying out in the evenings even after starting his new job.

When Margaret finally confronted him, it was as if they were re-enacting a confrontational scene in a tragic film.

"You're becoming a Hollywood cliché," she said one rainy morning sitting across from him at the kitchen table. "I found receipts from several restaurants in your suit pockets. There was a matchbook with a phone number and *Shirley* written inside the cover. I suppose I'll find lipstick stains on your collars and love notes in your pockets next." Her words were filled with ridicule rather than anger, which for Bernie was the worst kind of reproach.

She stood and walked to the kitchen sink, facing him with her hands grasping the counter behind. "You blame me, don't you?"

"Blame you for what?"

"For screwing up your career. For being a goddamn Red."

"You're not a communist."

"That's not the point! I was implicated. My friends and others I worked with were smeared too."

"That's not at all what this is about, Margaret."

"What *is* it about then? You don't love me anymore?"

"You know that I love you. It's not a question—"

She threw the telltale matchbook, hitting him. "I don't know who you are anymore!"

He stared blankly at his coffee cup. "That makes two of us."

"If you decide to continue with the same sad formula plot, you'll need to write me out of your script."

He knew that she was serious. She would pack his suitcase and leave it outside the locked front door.

Despite this, he continued with his escapades. It was as if he was addicted to guilt and self-reproach.

The night before JFK was shot, Bernie was having dinner with yet another young woman. He thought of taking her to the Sunset Inn, but instead sent her home in a cab. That night, he confessed everything to Margaret and begged her forgiveness. She told him that he was on probation.

The months following JFK's assassination were dark, especially for Margaret, who was devastated. As a representative of SAG, she had met JFK and his brothers several times at the Biltmore Hotel downtown. Bernie, remorseful and lonely, understood the shock she must have been experiencing, and he devoted himself to comforting her. A reconciliation gradually developed between them.

The loss of the young president had pushed the country—and Hollywood—into changing, due in part because JFK had inspired the younger generation. Films became grittier, taking on realistic, controversial subjects. Bernie was happy to find that his talent was once again in demand. He began working on a film adaptation of Tennessee Williams' *Night of the Iguana*. The love life of the film's stars became a media sensation, though a much different film, "Mary Poppins," was the highest grosser that year.

Other potential projects began landing in his lap.

Aaron, their second child, was three when they realized they could afford a nanny. Margaret had taken time away from her own work and wanted to return.

They decided to take a weekend trip. Bernie proposed spending it at the Sunset Inn.

She laughed. "Why not someplace like Santa Barbara?"

He hugged her. "You know why."

They packed a bag and informed the nanny they would return Sunday evening.

The Hideaway Lounge had been closed for a number of years. Sadly, it was boarded up now, its neon sign dark. Bernie had reserved Room 16. The manager mixed up the booking, but was able to exchange reservations with an out-of-towner.

The room's drapes were dingy, the furniture decrepit and towels thinner than they remembered. Even so, inspired by memories of their first times together, they spent most of the weekend in bed.

The manager gave Bernie a sly smile when he returned the key to the office. "I hope you enjoyed your weekend."

"Actually, my wife and I met here. At The Hideaway Lounge."

"Yes, the bar. That was before my time."

"It had a great bartender. He made the best Manhattan in LA."

"I guess nothing lasts forever, right?"

Bernie eased Margaret out of her hospital bed.

She sat at her long-abandoned vanity, brushed her hair, and with shaking hands applied a bit of makeup. He helped her with the lipstick. She directed him to find the dress she wanted to wear. "It should be in the back of the closet. I kept it. It's the one I wore for our wedding."

He helped her put on the tailored peach suit, now several sizes too large for her shrunken body.

The Sunset Inn had fallen even further from grace since their last visit, a tarnished relic. The Hideaway's neon sign had disappeared entirely. Bernie saw several Latino men, day workers by the looks of them, entering and leaving from where the bar had once been. He didn't recognize the manager, a man whose demeanor matched the motel's dreary appearance. As he returned to the car, one of the workers kindly asked if he could help him move Margaret to their room. Bernie thanked him, but shook his head. He needed to do this by himself.

Room 16 had aged with the motel, as he and Margaret had together aged. The sagging curtains, stained carpet, and strong odor of cleaning agents made him wonder for a moment if it had been a mistake to come here.

He helped Margaret settle onto the bed. She smiled faintly before he went back to the car to retrieve the suitcase that contained her special pillow, two highball glasses, a shaker containing the Manhattans, and the bottle of pills.

This had to be done correctly. He made her as comfortable as possible, propping her head up on the pillows so that she could more easily swallow.

He counted out the pills, then placed the white disks into two piles on the lamp table. With trembling hands, he poured out the drinks and handed a highball glass to Margaret. They would need water later to take the pills.

ROOM 16

Aaron Lauer checked in on his parents daily since his mother's diagnosis. His father had sounded strange on the phone yesterday, as if his usual anxious concern had been entirely wiped away. Something wasn't right.

He rang the bell, only a formality, and opened the front door with his key. "Dad?"

He walked into the den, where his mother's pill bottles were arranged in ordered rows on the night table. Two seemed to be missing. Missing too was his mother from the bed where she had been confined for the last many months. Had she been rushed to the hospital, his father too distressed to remember to call him?

The phone he had purchased for his father lay on top of the chest. Next to it sat an envelope addressed to him and to his sister, Emily, in his dad's neat handwriting. He tore back the seal and scanned the contents, breaking out in a panicky sweat as he read the letter's last paragraph.

Your mother and I met sixty years ago and knew we were destined to spend our lives together. It was miraculous, really, how we found one another. We've decided to take our leave in the place where our lives together began. We've not made this decision rashly or in despair. We love you and are very proud of both of you.

His father's meaning was clear. But where would they have gone?

Lodged in his head among the stories his folks often told

was the motel where they had spent their honeymoon. His father had never failed to point out the location whenever they drove by. Emily and he had even made a standing joke about their parents' thrifty choice. He searched desperately for the motel's website on his phone, but only managed to find the number after being directed to a generic travel site.

A gruff-voiced man who identified himself as Edward answered. "The Sunset Inn. Can I help you?"

"This is Aaron Lauer. My parents are Bernard and Margaret Lauer. Did they check in earlier today?"

"I'm sorry, but I can't give out any information about our guests."

"I'm their son, dammit! My parents are elderly, and my mother is very sick. I think they must have come there."

The manager's resistant tone shifted to unease. "They arrived a few hours ago."

"Please check on them for me," pleaded Aaron. "I just found a note from my father that says they plan something— something terrible at the motel."

"Hold on, sir. I'll check on them."

Edward sprinted to Room 16. "Damn it! Please, not here." He pounded on the door, calling out to the couple. There was no response. He fumbled through his collection of keys and found the master, turning the bolt lock and throwing the door wide open.

The couple lay unmoving on the bed. Both were on their sides and facing one another, their arms entwined. Light from the night table's lamp illuminated the woman's white hair and forehead, leaving the man's face in shadow.

Edward averted his eyes for an instant, embarrassed to

witness these strangers' intimacy, though he realized something was terribly wrong. He rushed to the bed and held the woman's wrist.

There was no pulse. He placed two fingers against the man's neck, his pulse alarmingly faint.

Edward reached into his pocket for his phone, but he had forgotten it. He grabbed the phone's receiver from the night table, sending a pill bottle tumbling to the floor, and dialed 911.

"Hello. This is the manager at the Sunset Inn on Hollywood. I've found two people in Room 16. I need an ambulance."

"Are you with them now?" asked the dispatcher.

"I'm in their room."

"Is a drug overdose involved?"

Edward picked up the empty pill bottle. "I believe so."

He answered the standard list of questions and dashed back to the office. Taking two deep breaths, he informed the son, "Your parents aren't responding." A half-truth to spare the distraught man. "I've called 911."

"I don't understand. I just talked with them yesterday." Lauer's voice cracked. "I'll be there as soon as I can."

Edward rushed back to Room 16, startled again by what he found. He heard a siren blaring from the boulevard. Emergency vehicles cruised Hollywood's mean streets 24-7 responding to the area's countless emergencies. He hurried to the entrance and watched as an ambulance inched its way through knotted, uncooperative traffic. Veering across three lanes, it bounced into the entrance, its siren filling the parking court with ear-splitting blasts.

The paramedics pulled tactical bags and an oxygen tank from the back of the ambulance. Edward pointed, and they hurried inside. After checking each victim, they administered

Naloxone and oxygen to the old man.

Edward hovered at the doorway. One of the paramedics removed her mask and shook her head. "They're both gone."

A police cruiser arrived, its flashing red and blue lights reflected in the motel room's windows. As two officers walked toward Room 16, a white Prius entered and braked to a lurching stop. A man with curly hair and dark-framed glasses rushed out to follow them.

"Are my parents in there?"

The officers restrained the man and asked Edward to escort him to the office. An unmarked black sedan had pulled up, adding to the tangle. A man in an ill-fitting suit appeared from it, narrow-shouldered and exceptionally tall, and strode toward the officers.

Edward watched their interaction from the open office door, Aaron Lauer pacing behind him. "I'm Detective Parker. I'll be taking over the investigation from here, fellas. I need one of you to stay, and one can leave."

The two cops stared at one another as if mentally tossing lots. The younger one shrugged and climbed back into the patrol car, presumably on the way to Dunkin' Donuts to celebrate his lucky break.

"Fill me in," ordered Parker, loosening his gray tie.

The uniform cleared his throat. "A couple in their eighties. It appears to be a double suicide. We found two empty bottles of sleeping pills. Their son is here." He pointed toward the office where Aaron Lauer was slumped in a chair with his head in his hands.

"Was the son here when it happened?"

Edward spoke up. "He just arrived. Said he found a suicide note."

"And you are?" asked the detective.

"Edward Sykes, the motel manager. I found them in their room."

Parker shot him a swift assessment and turned back to the officer. "I want to talk with the son. No one is to enter or leave until I say so."

He pointed a finger at Edward. "I'll need to ask you some questions too. Don't go anywhere."

A white station wagon pulled into the driveway and stopped short, blocked by other vehicles now crowding the asphalt. The two occupants opened up the back, pulled on white hazmat suits and grabbed black cases, talking briefly with Parker before they entered the room.

The detective advanced into the office and approached the son, flashing his badge. "I'm Detective Parker. I'm very sorry about your parents."

Lauer raised head, torment marking his face. "I don't get it. Mother's pain was being managed."

Parker sat in a chair next to him. "She was sick?"

"My mother has—had—myeloma. Bone cancer."

"Did you have any reason to think they were going to do this?"

"None at all. Dad seemed resigned to the fact that Mother wasn't going to get better. They both seemed to be at peace with that." He broke into a gasping sob. "Her condition had brought us all closer together."

The detective raised an eyebrow. "So, there were family issues?"

"I haven't called my sister yet. I don't know how I'm going to tell her."

"You mentioned something to the manger about a note they left. Do you have it?"

Lauer searched his jacket pocket and came up empty. "I

must have left it at the house."

Parker placed a hand on the man's shoulder. "We'll need to conduct a search at your parent's residence. I'll have some further questions, but I can save them for tomorrow. Here's my card. You're free to go after you leave your contacts."

Aaron tightened his grip around the card until it buckled. "I'm not leaving until my parents leave."

"That's perfectly fine." Parker strode across the asphalt court, where a ragtag group of curiosity-seekers had gathered. He barked at them, quickly dispersing the crowd.

Edward was left alone with Lauer. He offered him a drink, but the man shook his head. "I'm going to the car. I need to call my sister."

Edward poured Scotch into a glass and bolted it down. It had been terrible to discover a fine old couple like that. It wouldn't have been as bad with some of the motel's guests. He had often fantasized about offing a few himself.

Parker's gravel voice carried into the office. "Those prescription bottles... contact their doctor... and bag those drinking glasses for the lab." His voice grew fainter as he moved deeper into the room. "There are no belongings in the suitcase. But look at this photo taped to the wall. What do you suppose that's about?"

Edward had noticed a photograph above the bed himself, but was too shocked at seeing the couple to make anything of it.

The detective's recital continued: "There's no apparent evidence of any violence...Unless, of course, someone tried to make it look like suicide. I'm going to treat this as a possible homicide until forensics completes its investigation."

Edward shook his head, sure that no one had entered after the couple arrived.

Parker appeared outside the door and gave orders to the officer trailing behind. "I want the driveway taped. No one is to enter or to leave." He shook his head. "What really gets me is why a nice elderly couple like that would choose a shithole like this to off themselves?"

Edward automatically bristled, although he couldn't argue with the detective's assessment of his crumbling domain. He watched as the man searched about the premises, frowning into the late afternoon sun. He was like a bloodhound, nosing out a still fresh trail, sniffing at a clue. He surveyed the parking court's perimeter and all the rooms before taking long-legged strides toward the office.

"Where has the son disappeared to?"

Edward pointed to the Prius where Aaron Lauer was talking on his phone.

Parker cleared his throat, his prominent Adam's apple bobbing. "So, Mr. Sykes, I need you to tell me everything you know about the incident, everything you heard and saw."

"Do you mind if I sit down? This has all been pretty upsetting."

"Be my guest." The detective fished a pen and a pad from his jacket pocket. "What time did the couple check in?"

It was at 11:10. It's right in there." Edward indicated the motel's register on the counter. Parker examined the entry and scribbled something on his pad. "How did he pay for the room?"

"With a credit card." Edward sighed inwardly, relieved that Lauer hadn't used cash. He might have been tempted to pocket it. Any investigation would discover the disparity in the day's receipts.

The detective leaned against the counter, crossing a bony knee over the other. "Did they make a reservation?"

"Mr. Lauer called three days ago and asked for Room 16 for one night."

"Did you think that was strange? Requesting a specific room."

"People do sometimes. He said that he and his wife were taking a trip."

Parker frowned grimly. "Some trip." He drummed his pen against the pad. "How did Mr. Lauer appear when he checked in? Did he seem upset in any way?"

Edward fidgeted in his seat. "Not that I could see. He was courteous and well-dressed in a nice sport coat and slacks. His wife was well-dressed too in an old-fashioned pastel dress. But I could see that she was sick."

"What do you mean?" Parker splayed his long fingers in the air as if pushing his questions forward.

"She was very thin and seemed weak. She leaned against him all the way to the room."

At first, he had assumed the man was a john, and clearly risking a stroke, considering his advanced age. Curious, he had looked outside and was surprised instead to witness the elderly guest helping a frail-appearing woman out of the car.

"Tell me once again. What motivated you to check on them?"

"Their son sounded desperate on the phone. He told me that his father had left a suicide note. I ran out to knock on their door. There was no answer, and so I opened up. I could see that it didn't look right."

The detective raised his eyebrows into two dark question marks. "How so?"

"They were lying on the bed but their postures were strange, somehow unnatural. I called to them but they didn't move. That's when I checked their pulses, and called 911."

"You get a lot of lowlifes staying here."

It wasn't a question. The man was throwing him a curveball, maybe to catch him off-guard. "We get all types. Not everyone can afford expensive LA hotel rates."

"You often rent rooms by the hour, correct?"

"Most people stay for a night or two." He could feel beads of sweat beginning to develop on his forehead.

Parker fished in his jacket pocket. "I want to show you something. "This was taped on the wall above their bed."

He handed over a faded black-and-white photograph. It was clearly from another time, with old-fashioned scalloped edges around its border. The image showed a young couple standing next to one another. She was smiling and holding a highball glass up to the camera. The young man appeared surprised, or possibly annoyed.

On the wall behind them, a sign spelled out a name—Hideaway Lounge.

Does anything about this look familiar to you?"

Edward shook his head. "I can't say that it does."

"Look at the date," ordered Parker, pointing to the black print on the ragged border. March 1956. "I'm asking again. "Do you know anything about this Hideaway Lounge?"

Nothing." His throat caught. He and Rogelio, his partner in crime, had maintained the abandoned space as an income-producing crash pad for dayworkers until two weeks ago when news broke that the property was to be sold. They had hustled the illegals out, but the room was still littered with remnants of the men's occupancy.

The detective peered at him with keen precision. "I'd like to get in touch with the owner. Maybe he can provide more information."

"I doubt it. He's in his eighties and isn't so sharp anymore."

Actually, old Avery still seemed pretty keen. And he had often waxed nostalgic about the motel during its glory days, especially about the long-closed Hideaway Lounge.

The detective held a glint in his eyes, as if he felt that he was on to something. "I'll need the owner's phone number along with the merchant copy of Lauer's charge."

Edward's underarms were leaking. The man was a persistent bloodhound. If he requested entry to Room 1, he might link the crash pad to the Hideaway Lounge, and report what he discovered to the owner.

He considered providing Avery's phone number with one digit off to buy some time, but this would only raise further suspicion.

Parker stuffed the phone number and charge receipt into his sport coat's pocket. "That's all I have for you now, unless you have anything more to add. I'm sticking around until forensics finishes up, and the ambulance arrives to take the bodies to the morgue. The parking lot will have to remain taped off until our investigation of the premises is finished."

The detective stopped in front of Room 1 and attempted to peek though the tightly-drawn curtains. He then tried the locked doorknob before stopping at Aaron Lauer's car to talk.

Edward fumbled under the counter and poured himself a generous measure, and swallowed it in two quick gulps. He vacillated between resentment and remorse. Why had that couple chosen his motel to end their lives? And would it have ended differently if he'd taken more interest in their welfare?

But right now, he needed to get Room 1 cleaned up. He dialed Luisa's number. Rogelio, his partner in the room's enterprise, answered.

"Is Luisa with you?"

"She's working late at the restaurant tonight. I'm looking

after her kids." The man laughed. "I think she's trying to make an honest man of me."

"When does she get back?"

"Not until after midnight. You want me to leave a message for her or not?"

"Listen, Rogelio. There's been an incident at the motel. Two guests have died and the place is swarming with cops. I want you to get a truck and empty out that damned crash pad tonight, or both of our heads are going to end up on a platter."

"I don't know, man. Luisa and I had planned to spend the night together."

"I'm not asking you. Find a neighbor to take her kids. And tell Luisa I need her to come in early tomorrow morning to get that room spotless. Tell her we'll pay extra."

Edward slammed down the receiver. As he poured himself another drink, an ambulance pulled in. Two individuals appeared and removed a gurney from the back, wheeling it into Room 16. They emerged minutes later with a sheet pulled over a body.

Aaron Lauer lurched out of his car as they brought out the second body. Buried under its white covering, it barely made any impression at all.

FLAMES

Edward woke up to the scent of smoke tugging at his nostrils. Groaning, he slid out of bed and peered through the open office windows. A smoggy cloud drifted over the parking court, fumes leaking from under the door of Room 8. Another day, another emergency for a manager to manage.

He pulled on his sweatpants and grabbed an extinguisher, calling his familiar friends at 911 as he rushed outside. Instinct directed him to warn the guests, but it might cause panic among early morning sleepers. He'd first try to get the situation under control.

He pounded on the overheated door. "Mr. Reitman, open up!"

No response. Reitman must be fast asleep with his bevy of painted pals, he thought.

He used the master key to enter, but finding the chain lock engaged, he kicked until it broke away. Flames were leaping from a trash can and spreading to the carpet. Its synthetic fibers gave off an acrid fug. He covered his nose and mouth with his arm, and pulled the extinguisher's pin, squeezing the trigger to send foamy retardants to put out the blaze.

Through the dense fog of smoke, he could make out figures lying on the nearest bed. He charged toward them, until up close, he saw they were Reitman's life-size dolls, their painted expressions permanently frozen into calm composure.

He lurched toward the other bed and, fumbling, grasped

actual human flesh. He nudged, poked and prodded. "Wake up, Reitman.! You need to get out of here!"

The man wasn't responding. Edward cursed and grabbed him by the shoulders, dragging him off the bed and out the door.

He dropped the man onto the asphalt, where, boxer shorts drawn to his knees, he came to and stuttered, "What the hell are you doing? It can't be checkout time yet."

"Your room was on fire. You were suffocating."

The man's eyes opened wide and in a raw panic, croaked, "All my girls are in there! You have to get them out!"

"What the hell are you talking about?"

"You must save them!" howled Reitman. "They'll die in there." He stared with terror-stricken eyes into the smoke still rolling out of the room.

Edward's throat felt as if he'd swallowed thistles. "They're already dead. They're dolls, not women."

Reitman stared at him blankly and shook his head. Wheezing, he wrenched himself up from the pavement and began crawling toward the room on his hands and knees.

Edward grabbed him from behind and tossed him back onto the pavement. His sobbing guest thrashed his arms and legs wildly about, like an upturned beetle.

A collection of half-dressed residents had been drawn outside by the uproar. A john in boxer shorts stared from his door. His date, who appeared to be wearing nothing at all, peeked from behind him. A woman in pink hair rollers clung to her aqua-colored bathrobe, shaking her head in silent fascination. Her brawny-shouldered neighbor from the room next door, her face plastered with makeup and wig askew, clutched a poodle. Edward made note that she hadn't paid a pet fee. Dragging on a joint, a shirtless young man in cargo shorts was recording the event with his phone,

Meanwhile, Reitman was pleading. "Please, you've got to rescue my girls!"

"This is insanity," thought Edward. Even so, he bolted inside and searched through the dense haze to find a polymer beauty lying prone on the bed, and carried her outside to reunite with her boyfriend.

"Betty! Thank God!" crooned Reitman. "But what about my other girls!"

Those who were watching urged the manager on, apparently believing the victims inside were living beings. Not one of them volunteered to help.

Edward staggered back to discover another weekend playmate sprawled on a chair. He seized her and fled outside, dropping another scantily dressed date next to Reitman, who gasped, "Rose! But where are Tif and Shirley?"

Edward stumbled back inside, hacking from the acrid stench of melted synthetic carpeting and ancient layers of lead-based paint. He discovered a sporty-looking survivor wearing cherry red lingerie, and cradled her in his arms. With his nose pressed against her forehead, he thought for one mad moment of his wedding night so many years ago.

"Tiffany!" The sooty groom hugged his buxom bride. "But where's Shirley? She must be fuming. She can't even tolerate cigarette smoke."

Edward limped back for what he vowed would be the very last time. He discovered Shirley wearing a prim expression and a plain nightgown, hands clasped on her lap as if waiting patiently to be rescued. Her savior emerged covered in ash and breathing unevenly. In the light of dawn, he detected a melted scar on her otherwise flawless cheek. It gave Shirley the aspect of a gun moll grazed by a stray bullet.

Reitman folded the sooty darling in his arms as a disorderly cheer rose up from the crowd. One onlooker, a cigarette hanging from his lips, shouted at Edward. "You're some righteous hero, bro!"

"Right on," confirmed his shirtless friend. "You saved those girls."

The woman with brawny shoulders sashayed up to Edward and whispered, "You can visit me for free in Room 6." The poodle barked in agreement.

A blast from a fire truck's claxon drowned out the acclamation, roaring into the driveway. Within seconds, the firefighters were performing another show for the guests, leaping from the truck like gymnasts and swiftly hauling a long firehose into Room 8 to give it a destructive dousing.

Two carrying oxygen tanks glanced askance at the four inert figures lying next Reitman. Emergency calls from the Sunset Inn were frequent, but they had never seen anything quite like this.

The captain told Edward they had discovered pools of melted wax from several candles. One of them seemed to have fallen into the trash can.

"Good thing you pulled your guest out in time. Chuckling, he added, "I guess you saved his blowup dolls too?"

"He begged me to do it," Edward grumbled.

The captain shook his head in disbelief. "It takes all kinds, I guess."

Edward wasn't sure if the man meant Reitman, or him.

A staticky voice escaped the engine's radio, saving further explanation.

"We have a four-alarm on our hands, men," shouted the captain. "Bathhouse on Ivar."

His company rolled the hose in place and clambered onto

the truck. It backed slowly out of the driveway and sped along Hollywood, its claxon assaulting the rare peace of Sunday morning.

Reitman was busy brushing the soot from the faces of his entourage.

Edward stood over him. "You burned yourself out of your room. You're going to have to find someplace else to stay."

"The girls are too traumatized to stay in town, anyway," replied Reitman. "I'm taking them home."

"Maybe you should take them to the ER to get them properly examined."

"That won't be necessary," the man answered, in all seriousness. He sauntered into the soaked, ash-filled remains of his room to collect whatever belongings survived, emerging several minutes later with his hair combed and wearing a scorched white shirt and pants splattered with wet soot.

Forever the lothario, thought Edward, as he watched his guest load his cortege into his car. Then, waving at no one in particular, he drove away.

The next morning, the digital edition of *The Hollywood Reporter,* in need of provocative filler for Monday's posting, published a short account of the incident:

Film World Destination's Fiery Inferno

Edward Sykes, manager of the Sunset Inn on Hollywood Boulevard, extinguished flames spreading through a guest room before rescuing its surprising occupants that included a bevy of blowup beauties that harken back to the motel's heyday of guests like Dorothy Dandridge and Betty Grable. Guests witnessing the incident hailed the manager as a hero. Sykes declined to be interviewed by our reporter. The Sunset Inn is soon slated for closure, another storied local landmark replaced by a strip mall.

The report included a photo of the manager carrying one of Larry Reitman's seductive girlfriends through a smoking doorway.

The office phone summoned him all that afternoon, but Edward ignored it. "What does it matter, anyway?" he muttered. The Sunset was closing down for good soon, anyway.

He had promised himself to stop drinking after meeting Darrisha, the recent guest who described her incarceration, her long battle to get clean, and her fight to be reunited with her daughter.

He eyed the half-empty bottle of Scotch under the counter. His pledge to quit would have to wait until another day.

REUNION

Alice stood in front of the motel, heat radiating from the sidewalk in shimmering waves. She loosened the top button of her silk blouse and peered into the parking court.

The Sunset Inn, its paint faded and stucco cracked, was several degrees beyond shabby. Cement planters stood at either side of the entrance, filled with soda cans, fast-food wrappers, and cigarette butts. Dried soil hugged the remains of what once could have been palms.

Two young men in torn jeans and tank tops strutted past, shouting into their phones. A woman wearing a rhinestone top and frayed, tie-dyed shorts, her bright yellow hair sashaying behind her, eyed Alice's navy-blue suit and sensible, low-heeled black pumps scornfully.

What had she hoped to accomplish by coming here? It wasn't as if they had ever spoken. They were strangers. He may not even want to see her.

She hadn't known of his existence until she was twelve and overheard her mother mentioning something about "my first husband" to a friend. She had only been a kid then, and didn't dare ask. Even so, a notion had entered her head. Her identity wouldn't be complete until she knew who this man was.

Years later, when Alice pressed her mother on the subject, Margaret responded obliquely. "I left your father a few months before you were born. That's all in the past. Why bring it up now?"

"Does he know about me?" asked Alice.

Her mother nodded. "I told him after I married your stepfather."

Alice needed to know something—anything—about him.

"I don't know why you should care. Gus raised you."

When she insisted, Margaret said, "Ed would have made a useless father. You've been better off without him." But she reluctantly divulged his full name, and hinted that he might still live in Los Angeles. "That's all I know."

Fearing the disappointment her mother had forecast, she delayed any attempt to find him. It wasn't until after graduating from college that she felt compelled to search. This blank space, this incompleteness in her life, she suspected, affected her relationships with men. She kept herself distant from them, almost against her will, moving from one boyfriend to another, as if always failing to find something of her phantom father in them.

An early Web search had yielded no information. She dug deeper and came up with two recent items. The first was an article from the *Los Angeles Times*. It reported that Edward Sykes, manager of the Sunset Inn, had found an elderly couple in their room, both dead from apparent suicide. Another, from *The Hollywood Reporter*, detailed Sykes' rescue of "an eccentric guest and his peculiar harem from a fiery inferno."

Both stories noted that the motel was slated for demolition. If she wanted to meet her father, she had better do it soon.

An academic conference she planned to attend was being held in Los Angeles. She would be in town for three days. She skipped the second morning's session and scheduled a Lyft to take her to Hollywood.

Now, fortifying her resolve, Alice marched into the parking court. Dangling from two rusty chains, a sign for the office showed a red arrow that pointed around the corner.

The asphalt was wet from a dousing, making the air cooler. She sniffed at the faint odor of burnt ash. Two Latina housekeepers pushed their carts between rooms and chatted in Spanish. A bare-chested man stood outside an open door, smoking a cigarette and leering at them, turning away when he saw her approaching.

Another man, balding and slightly pudgy, bent over a hose and wound it into a coil. Sensing her presence, he stopped and glanced up.

"Is there anything I can help you with, miss?" he asked, squinting in a shaft of sunlight illuminating his face.

Alice always believed that she would recognize him instantly. His eyes were deep gray like her own. His nose, like hers, carried a slight tilt.

She calmed herself by drawing her breath in, and then slowly letting it out.

"Yes… I've been searching for you."

He dropped the hose and stood to his full height. "I'm sorry. Do I know you?"

Her heart was racing. "Not exactly. But you knew my mother, Margaret."

He gazed at her quizzically for a moment, until, at last, his eyes lit up.

"You're Alice, aren't you?" He broke into a broad smile and advanced toward her, his arms opening wide in welcome. "I've always hoped we would meet.

ROYAL FLUSH

Toni sat apart from us in the dressing room while I played gin rummy with the local girls in the show. She was staring into the hazy mirror, pouring shots and lighting up Tareytons. If the audience could have seen her then—wig tossed onto the table, her matted hair stuffed under a net, her tits sagging and makeup smeared —they would have demanded refunds.

She had been performing her "farewell tour" for a very long time. I wondered how much longer she could go on. It had been over a decade since Toni justified star billing, but she still managed to work a room with her impersonations. If no one looked or listened too closely, that is. Time had killed her looks, Scotch and cigarettes had murdered her voice. She lip-synched all her songs now, and her repertoire is antique, those standard divas, Streisand, Garland and Holiday. I had suggested newer material—Beyoncé for instance, or even Rhianna—but her ambition had folded like a bad hand of cards.

Those last shows had been utterly disastrous. Toni got destroyed in Chicago by that bitch who threw shade with her vicious review. In Milwaukee, she was the warm-up act for ladies' mud wrestling.

Earlier that evening, I had repaired one of her old gowns that should have been dumped in last century's rag bin. Toni had recently discovered a rat's nest wig that I'd tossed in the garbage. Its chestnut strands were permanently matted, and the netting was exposed in telltale patches. She had plopped it onto her head anyway. I tried to grab it off her, but she swatted my hands away.

Whenever the phone rang, I answered in my best lady-like voice, with an uplift at the end. "Toni Macy's dressing room."

A craggy voice full of mucous demanded, "Cristal. It's Max! Is Toni there?"

I mouthed, *It's Max,* and handed her the phone.

"What do you want now?" she moaned.

Her voice, once a sweet whisper, had grown rough. A critic had once described it as "a broken muffler over gravel." She screwed up her face while listening, bobbing her head up and down before she hung up with a loud snort.

"What did Max want?" I asked.

"He claims the Cameo Club is reopening. He must be off his rocker." Her puffy eyes searched the makeup table. "Where did I leave my drink?"

I didn't know this until two days later, but Max had only asked about Toni because he wanted to speak freely with me in private.

Max is, or rather was, Toni's agent. He is eighty and real old school, from a time when agents were a New York fraternity like the Mafia. Typecast for a 1940s B movie. Jewish, bald and pasty-faced, and as straight as they come. A cheap cigar permanently hangs from his mouth. Toni calls it his substitute dick.

He still wears those same dreadful suits, and I mean the very *same* suits he wore thirty years ago. He claims that the stains on his ties come from matzo ball soup. I tease him they're from bacon grease. He also claims that he was once the best in the business, which is as truthful as a drag's padding. He did miraculously manage to find himself a winning cheesecake with Toni, though. But that was decades ago.

Max never just talks, but shouts as if hawking secondhand goods on the street. And believe me, honey, in our circle of bitchy queens, I've heard plenty loud.

Whatever the man's faults, this queen is grateful to him for introducing me to books. And I mean good books, like *David Copperfield* (not the magician) and *Madam Bovary* (not the kid's book about pigs). I'd like to see those two stories appear in a single book sometime. I can't begin to tell you how much education and pleasure I've gotten from reading during those stretches of boredom between shows! After all, a girl can play cards or listen to Toni repeat tired tales about her stardom on the sequin stage for only so long.

The Cameo Club was located on a seedy stretch of Ninth Avenue near Times Square. Hell's Kitchen rightly deserved its name back then, in the early '80s. Liquor stores, smoke shops, porno dens, and single-room occupancies packed with pimps, pushers and hookers. Gays had finally stopped mourning the Death of Disco, but AIDS was making its horrible runway march. At the club, however, the girls still tucked in and carried on.

The Cameo, with its dusty red velvet curtains, stained flocked wallpaper, and stiletto-pitted floor, was as faded as a sixty-year-old drag queen. But at night, it still managed to offer a certain pretentious glamour. It had been a straight piano bar in the 1950s, until the queens started arriving with their fabulous entourages and drove them out. The club was forced to close for a short time after one of the girls sunk a knife into her cheating boyfriend's chest. The straights didn't return when it reopened, but the queens kept queuing up. There weren't many places for us back then, even in *tres gay* New York.

Max, as he often told the story, happened to stumble into the club one night after the opening of a play that included a bit part for one of his clients, a dreamy-looking hunk whose picture had just been featured in *Time Out*. During intermission, half the audience fled for an early dinner at Jo Allen. Those who stayed snickered during the second act's serious bits, and wisecracked over the actors' earnest lines.

Max stuck it out until curtain, and then sneaked backstage to offer false encouragement to his young newcomer. What he really wanted, though, was a stiff drink. He stepped around the corner to the nearest watering hole, the Cameo Club. He remembered getting a tip from a colleague recently about a talent there named Toni Macy.

He ordered a Dewar's and glanced around the bar. Faux gals in every direction, a deck full of queens. Two numbers on his right, sporting horrid Woolworths wigs and botched beard lines, were dishing insults. The bruiser on his left was sizing him up. In a deep baritone, she offered to provide him "massive peanut butter" if he cared to buy her a drink. He figured the agent who had tipped him off must have wanted to play a practical joke at his expense.

Yours truly was at the club that night too. I had arrived in New York only a few weeks earlier. On a Greyhound from Purdue, Alabama where I was known as Chris. I discovered the Cameo Club on my very first night in town. Dressed in my worn Levi's, a flannel shirt and a three-day-old stubble, the patrons assumed I was rough trade. But I knew that I had found my new home. I changed my name to Cristal that night and went shopping the next day.

I took a job as a dishwasher at a Greek place that ignored every health code in the city. I was generally not bothered by anyone there, except by the owner, who spouted invectives in

Greek about how slowly I scrubbed his pots to protect my nails. I was a scullery maid up to cherry pie in grease and soapy water, attacking towers of dirty dishes every day. At night, however, I came back to my room to rinse my bare essentials and slather myself with scented lotion. I steamed-pressed my only gown and fussed with the wig I had purchased at a moving sale on Tenth Avenue. I sashayed my tired ass into the Cameo nearly every night, a pretend princess living in my own make-believe fairy tale.

I always arrived unfashionably early to claim a chair near the stage. By the time I made a dash to the ladies' room and ordered my drink, girls in glitter were pouring into the place. I was so madly jealous of their fabulous wigs, feathers, and furs! I must have looked busted with my estate sale wig and Goodwill gown. I was still learning to walk in heels, tottering like a toddler. But since no self-respecting queen ever wore flats with her gown, I exchanged them for stilettos in the ladies' room, and prayed I would make it back to my seat without diving headfirst into a gaggle of empresses.

On the evening Max came into the club for the first time, he was in mourning for his promising ingenue's theatrical fiasco and picturing his own career sinking lower than a showbiz alcoholic's. In his own butch way, he could be as dramatic and self-pitying as any queen. He intended to make a beeline for the exit after only one drink. The Scotch burned in his throat as he plotted revenge on the joker who had sent him there.

A crusty-looking girl who resembled J. Edgar Hoover in drag was perched at the end of the bar, bellowing about how her thieving roommate had lifted her best rhinestone necklace. Two hot messes who would not have fooled an Amish tourist from Kansas slouched across from her. They were arguing over which of them was the fairest. Look in the mirror, he must have been thinking. That shoe will never fit. He had seen servicemen in Times Square far fairer. After tossing drinks in one another's faces, the two began throwing punches. The bouncer, a weightlifter with the high voice of a baby sparrow, ordered them to haul their asses outside.

Just as Max was about to hightail it himself, a man with a swerving hairstyle and wide lapels leapt onto the stage and grabbed the microphone. It was the club's owner, Larry Benson.

"Ladies and gentlemen! I hope I can safely say that you are all, indeed, ladies." The audience groaned, his joke falling flatter than a girl's wig in a heavy rain. "For all you Streisand lovers out there tonight, we have a very special treat for you later— Toni Macy, the Cameo Club's fabulous *chanteuse fatale*."

Unladylike whoops and hollers erupted amid shrieks and drumming applause.

"But first, let's bring on those tranny twins of tunes, Coupe Seville and Carmen Veranda!"

Theatrical moans greeted two elderly queens who appeared terribly more common than royal. Coupe Seville slipped on her train and was caught by the Carmen Veranda, who lost her pump. They began lip-synching to Loretta Lynn's "Some Kind of A Woman," exaggerating their mouths and out of sync with one another. For an unrequested encore, they mimicked the first bars of Lesley Gore's "It's My Party" before loud boos and shrill whistles forced the tacky twin travesties from the stage.

Max was strangely unaware that this was a comedy act. He had been determined to bolt out the door from the moment he entered the club, but something still held him back. He signaled to the bartender for a second drink just as Larry Benson's voice boomed over the PA.

"I see that our audience is growing restive. So, without further hairdo, I once again have the pleasure to present the lady that you've all been waiting for—the totally talented and forever divine, Miss Toni Macy!"

Toni was the reason, I confess, that I took the table closest to the stage.

The stage lights went dark, until, moments later, a single spotlight opened on an extended arm swathed in a long white glove covered with rhinestones. The music started slow and dreamy, like a gentle trance. An apparition sparkling from head to purple pumps stepped into the bright beam. Her voice emerged as a low whisper, sending the audience into rippling subdued sighs.

Toni elevated "No More Tears" into a hymn. She sang both parts, Barbra Streisand and Donna Summer. As the song's plaintive prelude moved into a pulsing disco beat, her voice turned on a dime, transforming a plaintive paean into a defiant rasping refrain. She shook her ass and ground her hips, twirling and dipping so low that she almost hugged the floor.

When she slipped the mic under her gown in one smooth move, the girl sitting next to me pretended a modest, "Oh, she didn't." A particularly enthusiastic queen attempted to stand on a table, but the heel of her stiletto missed, and she fell back onto her chair. But no one really seemed to notice. All eyes were on the stage.

Toni painted the house. She was fighting fierce in her flawless foam-green gown, wig styled into a crown of baroque curls, and seven-inch heels that I wished I too could someday wear. Older cutthroat cynical queen bees fussed with creases in their gowns and patted at their tipsy bouffant dos. Even the gay boys were jealous as hell.

The song slowed again, and Toni's voice grew mournful, pouring out loss and regret. She let the final note hang in the air, and, after a respectful pause, the entire audience jumped to their feet in applause.

Max was drinking Toni's performance up like a thirsty lush, realizing that he might still pull an ace from that night's bum deck. He imagined a future that might take him far from failed auditions and second-string flops. He started planning on making his move even before the first set ended. After Toni's second set, he forced his way backstage, despite Larry's threats to call the bouncers.

He performed his own song and dance for Toni. He told her how extraordinary she was, how successful he was as an agent and that she should chose his representation if she wanted to make a name for herself beyond the gritty streets of Hell's Kitchen. Toni pretended to be unimpressed.

Max remained undeterred. He would need to prove himself. He put the word out on his fabulous new find and nudged a few journalists to write reviews for the entertainment rags. Virgin patrons—downtown artists, gawkers from the Upper East Side, and even curious tourists—soon poured into the Cameo to check out the chanteuse who was getting all that attention.

Larry Benson loved the attention himself, and had no intention of letting Toni leave. Larry was an enthusiastic MC, but a lousy businessman and a tightwad. He never offered contracts to his performers. When a French entertainment magazine offered Toni a three-page photo feature and a club owner in Paris invited her to perform, she sunk a stiletto into Larry's chest and signed with Max.

But I'm getting ahead of myself. I'll back up a teensy bit, to the night that changed my entire life. Larry knew that his claim on Toni was coming to an end and he was angry. He ran around the club, barking orders at the waiters and laying into his bartenders for pouring too liberally.

I, of course, knew nothing about the situation. I had only parked my ass close to the stage, as usual. Toni was particularly fabulous that night, her makeup as fine as I'd ever seen it. She was hitting notes so high they could have rattled the chandeliers and melted the audience's mascara.

During her first set, she glanced once in my direction and appraised me, a gawky creature in a dime store wig who clearly adored her. I had positioned myself strategically, I admit. But imagine my surprise when Toni glided up to my table between sets and ousted the girl next to me with an imperious look. I'll never forget the whoosh of her cream-colored silk and organza gown as she floated onto the seat. I grew so excited that I nearly flooded my basement.

Our waiter, a femboy in tight black pants and white shirt unbuttoned to his navel, pranced over with a fresh drink and presented it to Toni. When she ordered another for me, the boy gave me the gimlet eye. She dismissed him with a wave of her hand, and sipped her cocktail while examining me silently. Nervous perspiration began to blossom on my face like a waterworks. I couldn't dare risk messing my makeup by blotting it with a cocktail napkin.

The waiter returned and slapped my drink down like a two-pint longshoreman. Toni's ruby lips turned up at the corners when I shot the same look of disdain that she had given him. Still, I could see that was she examining me up and down at the same time, clocking my every flaw—the uneven hem on my gown, my bargain basement makeup, the eye shadow that must look like paint on garage doors. I was sure the reek of my daytime job was eking through the knockoff Chanel No. 9 I had swiped from a Time's Square drugstore. I ran my tongue under my lips, trying to remove the lipstick from my front teeth. I hadn't yet learned the trick with Vaseline.

Whenever I get very nervous, I feel like throwing up. The prospect of dumping on Toni and pawing my way through that judgmental crowd to the ladies' room made me even more nauseous. I swallowed to keep it down and took sips from my vodka lime and soda hoping to hide any telltale odor.

"My dear Cristal," Toni purred as she removed her rhinestone gloves and placed them on the table. "That *is* your name, isn't it?" She stole an elegant nip from her drink, like a cat lapping cream. "I've just signed a contract with an agent. His name is Max Schaefer. He's promised to get me into the better clubs, and look for bookings outside of New York. He's arranged an appearance in—she whispered the word—Pa-ree."

She extracted a gorgeous silver case from her clutch and took out a cigarette, offering one to me. I told her that I didn't smoke. I hoped that refusing wasn't some awful faux pas.

"It's good that you don't smoke," she said. "It's bad for your lungs and it spoils the gowns." She drew on her gown-spoiler from a rhinestone holder, tilting her head while puffing perfect rings away from my face. She placed a perfectly manicured hand on my forearm, which was still painful from a hasty home waxing.

"I've been watching you here at the Cameo. You interest me. I believe you may have potential."

I was bewildered by her words. "But I-I've never been on stage."

"Oh, my dear, I don't mean performing!" Her laugh was high and musical, not really cruel. "You don't understand. I require someone to maintain my wigs and gowns, to keep my life in order."

My face must have burned bright red, even under all the

heavy foundation. I kept my mouth shut, afraid of making an even greater fool of myself.

"You're awfully young, and you have a lot to learn," she continued. "But I'm sure I can tutor you on what needs to be done."

I wasn't sure what exactly she was offering me. I only saw that my days of scrubbing greasy dishes and fending off a closeted Greek's advances might come to an end. I imagined sending I-told-you-so postcards to the folks back home from Paris, London, Los Angeles, and San Francisco.

Toni's eyes glittered with impatience. "Well, Cristal, do you want the position or not? I have a costume change and another show in fifteen minutes."

"Oh, yes, thank you!" I wanted to hug her, but she raised her hands to fend me off from mussing her.

"I'll take you on a trial basis. Let's see how things work out between us, shall we?" She cautioned me not to repeat our conversation to anyone, "There are snakes here eager to use the merest shred of gossip against me." She pulled her gloves up to a millimeter short of her elbows and stood from the table. "The first thing we need to do is work on that accent of yours. And you'll also need to learn to tuck properly."

Toni left as regally as she had come.

I was jubilant and numb, the room around me a blur.

My night had started with a whores' bath in a cracked, stained sink before cramming myself into a gown a size too small. And now, unexpected triumph. Considering the lousy cards handed me at birth, an abusive father and a mother who drank, I had been dealt a flush deck.

Nothing is as it first seems. I spent the first week in Toni's employ on my hands and knees scrubbing her dressing room floor with a nailbrush. But still, compared to Gyro Haven, I was in heaven.

"Honey, I started on my knees in a hell of a lot worse situation than this," she declared. "This is only a test of your fortitude." Her stage voice was like a purring kitten's, but offstage she was raspy, her laugh deep and throaty. She maintained an aura of flawless glamor in public but offered me her unadorned self, minus the gowns and the wigs, the lifts and the makeup. She often appeared tired and drawn, acted cranky and bitchy.

Max is quite a fabulist, but he kept his word with Toni. She began performing in some of the higher-end clubs around town, followed by guest headliner at Finocchio's in San Francisco. There were sold-out performances in Vegas with the promise of multiple tours in Europe.

In Paris, she appeared at the largest club in Montmartre, only two sinful blocks away from Sacre Coeur. The show was elaborate, involving several scenery and costume changes. She even had a pit crew who danced backup, French boys in cute sailor outfits and shirtless soldiers in tights. Male fans lined-up backstage, their cologne mixing with the scent of the flowers they carried. I had hoped to see more of the city, but the late-night hours left me too exhausted to do much more than lounge in the nearby cafés and take a tourist bus to see the landmarks.

Many clubs in the States catered to the same celebrities Toni impersonated. I could dish about the temperamental divas among them, but the stars were mostly good sports. They occasionally joined Toni on stage. I'll never forget the night of her duet with Streisand. "Somewhere" from West Side Story brought the whole house down.

There were endless male admirers, married men mostly, too

many with toupees, crowding the hallways to Toni's dressing rooms after her performances. They brought champagne and roses, perfume and gems, proposals and offers of ecstasy. It was my responsibility to tap the shoulder of the man she decided to invite inside. I made honeyed apologies to the others, even as I collected their offerings. Some propositioned me. I considered it a consolation prize for my pimping. I hustled these no-go gentlemen from my room early the next morning to enjoy a few hours of blissful reading with a cup of tea—what Toni called my "old lady habit"—before waking her in mid-afternoon with a cup of coffee and a fistful of aspirin.

She was always a hot mess from drinking and the night's wear and tear. No longer dusted, just bleary-eyed and busted. Five o'clock shadow showed through her clotted foundation, wig and silicone boobs hanging on the vanity, evening gown tossed on the floor.

We girls attract curiosity and sometimes bask in adoration. But we also endure insults and ridicule, or worse—violence from men who fear their attraction, loathing from women jealous of us.

We are artists of illusion who employ a paintbox of deceptions. Trompe l'oeil. No one was better at fooling the eye than Toni Macy. She became a star at a time when it required hard work to maintain a convincing artifice. It's easier now when any aspirant who scrimps and saves can appropriate the real thing. Hormones added or subtracted, a major snip here, a teensy tuck there, a matching set of boobs with a ten-year warranty.

Believe me, honey, when Toni appeared in all her hard-won glitter, more reflections bounced off her than from Tiffany's windows. But backstage, she suffered from fierce, destructive demons that no gloss and glamour could hide. The decline seemed to happen so quickly. Watching her fall was like seeing a goddess tumble from the clouds. Fascinating, but fatal.

At some point, I noticed that she no longer sipped like a lady but swilled like a longshoreman. Since my fate was attached to hers, I attempted to shore up the cracks in her foundation, the lapses in her lyrics. But during a particularly rough tour, with her bitch up and running, I have to admit that I sometimes took a certain pleasure in watching her downward spiral, the deshabille and the uninterrupted drinking.

Defeat is written all over Toni's face now. Whatever flame she once possessed has been extinguished after the humiliations she endured in those cow towns on Lake Michigan. She refuses to perform and no longer makes any attempt to dress. She shambles around the apartment in her bathrobe, carrying a drink in one hand and pinching her Tareytons with the other. She swears, hurling abuse like a murderous hag. After decades of impersonating others, she is most herself these days, a bitter old queen with a severe drinking problem.

Max called two weeks ago. The Cameo Club is re-opening at a fabulous new location on a gentrified block in Hell's Kitchen. Max, bless his retro heart, has negotiated with the club's owners to feature 'It's a Real Drag.' Mondays.

"It's too late in the game for Toni," he said. "But you know all the moves, don't you, Cristal? I've seen you secretly perform them when Toni wasn't looking. If you don't want to sing, you could lip-synch the lyrics. People are used to hearing everything recorded these days, anyway."

I told him that I needed to think about it.

"Don't take too long. The club opens for business in a month. I've promised a headliner for opening night."

I began working on my presentation the moment Max hung up, contemporary numbers for a new generation. Toni Macy's parlor maid was turning into Cinderella, a storybook queen at last.

After Max broke the news to Toni, she retired to her bed for several days. She refused to talk with me, but last Friday, she broke silence by asking me to play gin rummy. She dealt out the cards and attempted to cow me with a commanding look from across the table.

"I can't say I wasn't surprised you accepted Max's offer, Cristal. You've been waiting in the wings to replace me for a long time. But there's something you will never understand."

She tapped her chipped nails against the table top. "I was the Queen of Diamonds. The best you can hope for is to be the Jack of Clubs."

We came to the final hand. Toni was beaming. She set her cards down slowly, one at a time. "Royal flush! I win!"

Actually, I had won. The deck no longer belonged to her. It was mine.

It's strange and a little sad to witness her attempts to reign over my dressing room now. She grows furious when I tell her to stop smoking her filthy cigarettes. She is obviously boiling inside and very capable of sabotage. Sticking pins in my gown I won't discover until I'm onstage, then unplugging the sound system during my act.

To maintain the peace, I tell her that I wouldn't be where I am today if it hadn't been for her. Toni scrunches her face into a frightful frown and reaches for a drink and another cigarette.

A SWEET KID

"Brian and I are at our wit's end," my sister, Kat, confesses over the phone. "Justin tries to hide it, but we know he's smoking pot. Even at home. Who knows what he's doing when he's not here? We've threatened to send him to rehab this summer, but he told us that he'll run away if we do."

"Rehab seems awfully harsh, Kat. He's only seventeen." I remember how I too left home, only a little older than my nephew. I had just been outed at school and was convinced that our parents would send me to conversion therapy.

"Justin was so easy until this last year," she wails. "He was such a good student, getting As. But now he cuts classes and takes a bus somewhere downtown."

I'm tempted to remind her that not only did *she* smoke pot in high school but was also truant. Is it age, parenting, or both that makes my sister so tense and anxious? I miss her youthful sense of humor, her defiance and fearlessness.

"Brian searched his bedroom a couple of weeks ago," she continues. "He found a bong, a pipe, and a bag of weed. Fortunately, there was no other paraphernalia. Justin blew up when he discovered his room had been invaded. He taped a poster with a skull-and-crossbones on his door. They argue all the time now."

Unlike Kat, I never fought with our parents. I was good at pretense then. But I made up for it later. I had terrible drag outs with my two alcoholic ex-partners.

"Justin asked if he could visit you. What do you think?"

"I'm thinking." Living as a single man has, I confess, made me selfish.

"He loves you, Robert. He was so excited when he visited you last time."

I took time off from the gallery and we drove up to the Gold Country, then spent two days at Yosemite. He was a bright, sweet boy. But what do I know about teenagers, much less about my handle-with-extreme-care nephew?

"I know it's a lot to ask. You would be doing us a big favor."

Desperation rings in my sister's voice. Still, I'm tempted to say no.

"There's something you should know," she says. "Justin has just come out to us. Brian's having difficulties with it, but he's trying."

"So, you're asking me to be some kind of queer role model?"

"We really need a break, time to regroup."

"Okay, Kat. I just hope you're not expecting too much from this visit."

"You're a real lifesaver, Robert."

"I'll remember to wear my life jacket."

Kat doesn't laugh. "Justin spends half the night texting, and sleeps in whenever he gets a chance."

I once slept in late too, in my twenties, after dancing all night in the clubs. That was before life became virtual.

Justin, in shorts and hoodie, lopes up the terminal's walkway and stands before me. He unslings his backpack, neither smiling nor frowning. His dark hair, the tips frosted blond in the front, flops over his forehead, covering one eye.

I smile to conceal my apprehension. "Hello, Justin. It's

great to see you." I move to hug him but then hesitate and offer my hand, which he shakes with a strong grasp.

"Let's go get your bag downstairs."

He hefts his backpack onto one shoulder. "This is all I brought."

A biting wind assaults us on the pedestrian bridge to the parking structure. My nephew shivers and pulls up his hoodie. "I thought this was supposed to be California."

"It's our San Francisco summer. Remember how cold it was when you were here before?"

"Oh, yeah. I froze my ass off on the cable car."

Lights from a plane taking off reflect in my rearview mirror. The 101 is mercifully uncongested. Even after all these years, I'm still thrilled whenever I see the city's skyline appear, the skyscrapers downtown glowing, fog tumbling over the hills. I'm even starting to like the Salesforce Tower that resembles a phallus, an obvious statement from its owner. The building's gaudy LED display glows like a lightshow from Mount Olympus. Tonight, it features an anti-drug message, with diverse adolescents just saying no. Justin's eyes are glued to his iPhone's screen.

"Have you called your mother to let her know you're here? She'll be worried."

"Mom is always worried. That's her middle name."

"Then why not put her out of her misery?"

"I only text," he says. When I insist, he sighs and calls. "Hi, Mom. It's me. I'm in the car with Uncle Robert. Talk to you later."

Is he being curt, or was that voicemail? I don't ask.

I maneuver through jammed city streets and head up Market. Justin stares out the window at men in shorts and T-shirts crowding the sidewalks despite gale-force winds. At home,

Tigre greets us warily, peeking out from under the Chinese chest in the hallway. He's terribly territorial and not fond of visitors. At least he's not hissing, the prelude to a hunger strike and a pissing match.

Justin bends down to pet him, only sending Tigre deeper into the depths. "Isn't this the same cat you had when I visited last time? He must be a million years old now."

"He's only ten."

"That makes him fifty-three in human years."

My age. It might as well be a million.

We tread up the staircase, the metal steps ringing. My home office doubles as the guest room.

Justin races to the window and stares down at the city. "This is sweet. Baltimore isn't anything like this. I'm so fucking glad to be out of that shithole."

His vocabulary has expanded since I last saw him.

The next morning, I take Justin to work, a straight shot down Ashbury Heights to Seventeenth Street. My gallery used to be downtown on Geary Street until high-tech rents scattered us dealers across the city's forty-nine square miles. I was lucky to win the leasing lottery for a space at a former machine shop repurposed into a kind of art multiplex. There are six other galleries there, as well as meeting space and a café.

Dogpatch was once filled with light-manufacturing and working-class bars but is now chockablock with condos, vegan restaurants, and hip boutiques. I point out a few of the more interesting shops. Justin glances up from his phone and, feigning interest, nods. I park in my dedicated space—forget finding street parking anymore—and take the freight elevator to the second floor.

I switch on the gallery's spotlights, and Justin's eye, the one not covered by his thick thatch of hair, widens. "These graffiti paintings are mega cool!"

I'm cheered by his unexpected enthusiasm. "They're all by Nick Stone."

He was homeless for a few years but began painting after he stopped using drugs." I've decided to be instructive right out of the gate. "You can sit in my office with your phone while I change some of the artwork."

"I can help you," he volunteers.

"It's nice of you to help your million-year-old uncle." He either ignores or doesn't get my joke.

I pull one of Nicks' large canvases from the storage bin. The painting is bursting with brilliant fluorescent colors and overlapping images, among which are two anatomically identifiable men fucking. I'm caught off guard with my nephew standing next to me. But then, my sister must have known she was taking a chance when she sent her son to spend quality time with his gay-identified uncle.

We carry the painting into the main gallery and set it against the empty wall. I demonstrate a trick I use to install works at an ideal height, and have him pencil in the spots for two hooks. We attach the wire and step back. My new intern observes our handiwork critically and straightens it.

Patrick, my gallery assistant, bursts in and leads his bicycle into the back room. He's only a few years older than Justin, and once I make introductions, they fall into an easy conversation, trading arcane phrases I'm not hip enough to understand. After leaving Patrick a few instructions, I take Justin to lunch. Mexicali is always busy, but the food is terrific. My nephew wolfs down his carnitas, slurps two glasses of Coke, and orders flan for dessert. The sugar load alone would drive my health-conscious sister apoplectic.

He pushes his plate away. "If it's okay with you, I'd like to wander around for a while."

I debate whether I should let him out of my sight so soon, remembering how I wandered when I first came to the city, looking for trouble. "That's fine. I close the gallery at six, so please come back by then, or earlier if you get bored."

"Sure thing, Unc." He smiles antically and heads out while I take care of the bill, including a hefty tip for our handsome waiter.

At the gallery, a minivan arrives with expensively coiffed, middle-aged woman from Walnut Creek. I delegate Patrick to greet them while I hole up in the office and make a few calls before I make an appearance.

I can hear the visitors asking the usual questions. Where does the artist get his inspiration from? How long did it take him to paint it? Are posters available? The ladies are window-shopping, but their interest is sincere. There's always an off-chance that one of them might return with her husband to purchase something.

Six o'clock comes, with no sign of my nephew. I call his cell phone, but there's no answer. I try again ten minutes later, but he still doesn't pick up. He appears at 6:20, wearing a Duran Duran sweatshirt that might have been mine back in the day.

"Sorry. My phone went dead and I lost track of time," he explains. "There was some really dope stuff in that Goodwill down the street."

I don't like hearing him use that word. Dope.

He pulls out a pair of jeans from a shopping bag. They're ripped to shreds like those from the store around the corner that sell for $180. He unfurls several washed-out T-shirts printed with catchy phrases. Out comes another one emblazoned with

Queen in black Gothic font, along with a pair of bright magenta cargo shorts.

"I'm saving these for the Castro."

He's smiles at what must be the horrified expression on my face. The kid has a sense of humor, which is more than I can say for his uncle right now.

I toss a frozen cheese pizza in the oven for Justin and make a salad for myself. I've vowed to limit my intake of alcohol during his stay.

He gallops barefoot down the stairs, wearing one of his Goodwill tees. "Very cool crib, Uncle!" he enthuses. "The view is totally rad."

This house was a real mess when I had purchased it. Filthy carpeting. Leaky plumbing. Cat shit everywhere. But the place was cheap, the last bargain in San Francisco before real estate prices started going through the roof.

He grabs a soda from the fridge. "The hills here are so cool, like a roller coaster. Baltimore is so fucking flat."

"Damn!" I burn my fingers as I lift the pizza from the oven and nearly drop it.

He helps himself to a slice, rolling it up until it resembles an oozing, oversized joint.

"I remember how much you liked the roller coaster at Six Flags."

He pinches another slice. "I don't like theme parks anymore. They're for kids."

"What *do* you like to do now?"

He covers his mouth and burps. "Whatever. I'm just glad to be free."

When I was his age, I was free to have an after-school job at a pizzeria. I worked part time mowing lawns in the summer. On Saturday mornings, I took a bus across town to attend a painting class at the community center where I had my first sexual experience in the basement with a charismatic classmate.

Kat calls after dinner. "Justin just texted me. He said that you both had an awesome day together."

"Give me time, sis. There's two weeks to fuck it up."

My friends Ben and Leon are eager to meet Justin. I probably shouldn't have told them that he's just came out to his parents. I also made the mistake of mentioning something about drugs. They're good friends, but they can be campy and over-the-top. I've also invited Karen and Max to serve as buffers.

Ben, with Leon still fussing with his hair, arrive early and volunteer to help, which means drinking wine and watching me braise the chicken and prepare the risotto. Leon is supremely striking, with flawless dark skin and the longest eyelashes I've ever seen on a man. Ben is an exiled Midwesterner who shares unbridled tales of the couple's sexual antics, salting them with bawdy comments and peppering them with hair-raising details. I've asked them both to tone things down for tonight.

"Don't worry, dear," declares Ben. "Kids your nephew's age are spawned on the Web and social media. I'm sure he's been exposed to everything. Not that I can say the same about you."

"Where *is* the little drug addict?" asks Leon.

I wave a wooden spoon at them. "The topics of drugs and sex are verboten tonight."

Ben refills their glasses with Pinot Grigio. "But what else is there to talk about?"

"Justin's not some boy toy."

Relief troops arrive. Karen gives me a big hug. I met her

dancing at the Stud twenty years ago. She had given up on finding a partner while I was on my second. Max hugs me also, and hands over a bottle of Sauvignon Blanc. They met at some work-related event. It was love at first collation. Karen is exuberant, dark-haired and zaftig. Max is tall and good-looking in a blond god sort of way. He's the most gay-friendly straight man I've ever known, but that can sometimes inspire Ben and Leon to greater outrageousness.

Justin thunders down the stairs, his flip-flops flapping. He's wearing the magenta shorts and the *I Don't Play Games* tee.

I take him by the hand, as if leading a lamb to the slaughter. "Come meet my friends, Justin. This is Karen and Max."

He waves to Karen and shakes hands with Max.

Ben and Leon hover behind me. "It's good to meet you," chirps Ben. "We've heard so much about you," trills Leon. Not exactly the most reassuring thing to say to a sixteen-year-old with issues.

At dinner, as Justin scrapes capers off the chicken piccata, Karen and Max ask him safe questions. He responds politely as I invent his true answers in my head: Where do you live? In prison, with my parents. Where do you go to school? At Homophobic High. What's fun to do in Baltimore? Nothing.

Over dessert, Ben insists on talking about John Waters. "He's from Baltimore too, you know. I just love his films. Especially *Pink Flamingos*. He was in town recently. We went to see him at the Norse Auditorium. He's so wonderfully witty, and provocative."

I shoot him a cautionary look, but he patters on.

"He's incredibly hyper too. He must be on drugs all the time."

Justin appears to be underwhelmed by all this chitchat. He excuses himself from the table. "Sorry. I have to make a phone call."

"I bet he's calling his drug dealer," whispers Ben.

Leon arches his dark eyebrows. "Love those shorts."

"It's good of you to have him here," declares Max, changing the subject and saving me from exploding.

"My sister and brother-in-law needed a break. It's been a rough year for them."

Karen touches my shoulder. "If there's anything we can do, maybe fill-in for you sometime, let us know."

"We'd willing to help, too," echoes Leon.

I'm tempted to bite his nose off. I bite my tongue instead.

I'm leaving the house early with a list of Justin's favorite foods in my pocket. Veggie chips, turkey jerky, baby carrots, an expensive brand of organic soup as well as a kale and cranberry salad from Whole Foods Kat tells me he loves. The boy is spoiled. Back in my day, my sister and I ate whatever our mother served whether we liked it or not.

I make plans for the day while I wander the grocery aisles. It's been ages since I've driven to the ocean. I'll take Justin through Golden Gate Park and then to Ocean Beach. I'll show him those WPA-era murals at the Beach Chalet before we have lunch upstairs, at a window table staring out at the Pacific over crab cakes and a burger. Afterward, we can walk the trail along Land's End and check out Rodin's hunky sculptures at the Legion.

Back home, I shout out to him, but he doesn't respond. His bed is empty upstairs, the comforter tossed aside, the pillows indented from his sleepy head. The magenta shorts and tee he wore last night are wadded on the floor. I'm tempted to check for drugs, but instead I tromp back downstairs to find a scrawled note on the dining table amid the crumbs from last night's party.

I'm taking a walk. Back later. J.

At least he's getting some exercise. When I first came here, I walked everywhere from my grubby little studio apartment off Polk Street, exploring Chinatown and North Beach or dashing off to the Mission and the Castro. For me, it was a Technicolor urban *The Sound of Music* those first few years. I found plenty of opportunities to get into trouble, too. But instead of fretting, I heat up some of Justin's soup.

Ben calls and asks if he and Leon behaved themselves sufficiently last night. This is more a provocation than a question. "What are you two doing today?" he asks.

"I wish I knew. Justin has disappeared."

"Shall we organize a search party?"

Ben was once a Boy Scout. I don't take the bait.

I call Justin as soon as we hang up. He doesn't pick up. I follow up with a text then put on a meditation tape, attending to my breath and repeating an impossible mantra—peace is dwelling in me now.

The front door slams and Justin appears, wearing the torn jeans from Goodwill and the *Queen* T-shirt. I manage to intercept him before he reaches the stairs.

"I hope you're not going to interrogate me like Mom and Dad," he says, plopping down on my Danish lounge chair. He pulls at his frosted hair. His eyelids are half-shut. Are his pupils dilated?

I take a deep breath and temper my voice. "You have to understand, Justin, that I'm responsible for you right now. If something bad happened, how could I ever face your mother and father?"

"So, I guess you're actually worried more about yourself."

"That's not what I meant at all." How do Kat and Brian deal with this adolescent?

He glares at me, and mimics Leon. "We've heard so much about you." Then springs from the lounge chair and shouts, "Why is everyone always on my case!"

I decide it's best to let him cool down, sleep it off.

Kat calls as he tromps loudly up the stairs. "How are things going?"

"We've decided to have a quiet time at home today," I lie.

"I'm happy that things are going so well between you two."

"What are we doing today?" asks Justin, as if nothing happened between us yesterday. Clever boy.

We drive to the Castro where I treat him to a thirty-dollar haircut he thinks is "way cool." We then head out to Golden Gate Park. An Escalade pulls out from a spot in front of the Conservatory of Flowers, my parking angel hard at work. Tourists in pastel clothing mill around, taking selfies in front of the glass hall. Justin grimaces when I suggest we send a picture to his mom and dad. I stage him next to a flower bed planted with bright orange and yellow daffodils. He makes a funny face, his eyes buggy and his tongue sticking out.

"What's that?" he asks, pointing to the pedestrian tunnel that runs under JFK Drive.

It's the dank, urinous underpass I've avoided ever since seeing *A Clockwork Orange*. He runs inside, his hoots and hollers echoing off the walls.

He goes down on one knee and tilts his phone upward to snap a series of photos. I have to beg before he lets me see them. He has a good eye, using the tunnel's arched entrance to frame the bright, lively scene outside. I accidentally scroll to another series of photos. Justin, shirtless, sitting next to a young man whose arm is draped around his shoulder.

He grabs his phone from my hands and slips it into his pocket. I don't ask. I know he won't tell.

We hold our noses through the stinking underpass and emerge in front of a grove where colossal fern trees cohabit with elephantine mystery plants.

"It looks like dinosaurs could live here!" yells Justin.

He takes a video of two frogs humping on a lily pad. We wander past dense shrubbery where I once upon a time enjoyed dallying with other parkland flaneurs.

I've wanted to see the David Hockney show at the de Young before it closes. Thinking my nephew might grow bored with it, I lead him across the street to the Rose Garden. He quickly grows bored. We head back to the car and pass a clearing where several men in speedos tanned to mahogony lounge on the grass. Justin glances at them casually and moves on. As a young man, whenever I came across a scene like this one, the sexual implications would often overwhelm me, vacillating between apprehension and exhilaration.

We drive past the bison paddock, but there are no bison to be seen. As I maneuver the last curve on Kennedy Drive, we come face-to-face with the Pacific Ocean.

"Awesome!" exclaims Justin, nearly jumping from his seat.

I cross the Pacific Coast Highway and park in front of the seawall at Ocean Beach.

"I'll meet you down there!" He flips off his sneakers and scampers toward the water, spraying sand behind him.

"Be careful. There's an undertow!"

He wades into the water, gasping at the cold and yelling like a banshee as waves break over the hem of his shorts. I keep to the waterline until we reach the rocks at the end where we watch the surfers skim and tumble.

Justin lets me know he's hungry (when isn't he?). We race across the highway to the Beach Chalet, dodging traffic. I point out a few details in the lobby's mural, but he grows antsy and excuses himself to use the restroom. He appears a few minutes later. A man in a denim jacket behind him dashes out the front door.

"Did that man try anything with you?" I ask.

He peers at me as if I've totally lost it.

Patrick is managing the gallery again today. Justin and I can take the ferry to Sausalito. The view from the sidewalk café on Bridgeway is stunning, and my nephew is effusive. He tells me about sail-boating with his dad on Chesapeake Bay and about wanting to become a marine biologist. Kat has never mentioned that. At Surf's Up, he tries on a pair of "sick" boardshorts, and chooses two tees. I'm treating, and nix the one with *Cannabis Wave Rider* scrawled across the front.

We pass the Rogers Gallery. I had a brief fling with Ron Rogers years ago. We hug. He keeps eyeing my nephew a bit too archly, and we don't stay long.

Outside, Justin shoots me a sly look. "So, how do you know him?"

"Ron and I are in the same business."

"How many lovers have you had in your life?"

A middle-aged couple in matching baby blue jogging suits turn, and stare. My nephew slings his arm around my waist and feigns adoration. They appear alarmed.

"I know Mom told you that I came out to them," says Justin. "They aren't making that big a deal about it, not like they are about me smoking grass."

"Coming out is easier now than it was when I was your age."

"Mom said that you left home when you were still in high school. That must have been kind of scary, leaving your life behind."

"It was scarier to stay, and easy to make friends here."

"I bet it was easy to get drugs then, too."

"I don't think I should answer that."

We walk to a small park on the hilly side of Bridgeway and settle on a bench. The city across the Bay shimmers in the distance.

"When I was twenty-five, I almost got arrested for smoking pot in this park."

My nephew's eyes light up. "Really?"

"I was with a friend, and we decided to get high. We figured that no one would notice. Big mistake."

"What happened?"

"Someone passing by must have seen us, or smelled us, and reported it to the foot patrol."

"No way! That would totally weird me out."

"Fortunately, we saw them coming. My friend dropped the joint, and snuffed it out with his shoe. The officers demanded to see our IDs. My friend hid the joint with his foot the whole time."

Justin snickers. "What happened to you?'

"They made a big show of writing up a report for vagrancy, and escorted us to make sure we got back on the ferry to San Francisco."

"But pot is legal in California now. It's not a problem to smoke in public anymore, right?"

"It's still a problem if you're under twenty-one."

"Practically everyone at my school smokes. Mom and Dad act like it's the end of the world. They guzzle a bottle of wine every night.”

“Drugs have the biggest impact when you’re young, and it’s definitely addictive.” I’m beginning to sound like a TV ad, so I change the subject. “What’s this about you skipping school?”

“Sometimes I just want to chill with my friends.”

I recall the photograph of Justin sitting next to the young man. “You may be sacrificing your future in ways you can’t imagine. Why *do* you smoke pot, Justin?”

He glances around the park, as if searching for an answer that’s hiding in the bushes. “It makes me feel normal, and helps me get through things.”

“Pot may help you relax, but your brain will keep compensating for it. When you’re not high, your stress level increases, and you need more THC to feel good.”

I really should go on the teen anti-drug lecture circuit.

“You smoked when you were my age. And you left home too.”

“The town your mother and I were raised in was full of people who hated fags. I would have been persecuted if I’d stayed.”

“I’m being persecuted too! Mom and Dad carry so much shit in their heads. They ground me for no good reason, and—

“They worry about you. That’s what parents do.”

“I hate them. They’re always colluding against me.” He slams his palm against the bench.

“It’s actually compulsory for seventeen-year-olds to hate their parents. But they’re still entitled to have a say in your life. You don’t realize how fortunate you are. They’re trying to support you.”

They wanted him to spend time with his gay uncle, for god sakes.

“What if I bought some pot to share with you?” He slips

me a sly look.

"That's not going to happen."

"Have you ever tried opiates or meth?"

I don't like where this conversation is going. "Meth, opiates, and cocaine—they're killers. Promise me you won't do any of that stuff."

He holds his hand to his heart. His attempt at an innocent expression reminds me of a jaded Caravaggio saint.

We head back to the ferry landing. A group of men with soft Southern accents are waiting at the dock, joking and camping. The couples among them are holding hands. Justin, bridling from my lecture, observes them sullenly.

The passengers board two at a time, like unicorns entering Noah's Ark.

I need to catch up with work today, and accept Karen and Max's offer to spend time with Justin. They suggest lunch and a hike afterwards that might satisfy Justin's wanderlust.

At the gallery, Patrick hands me a list of potential collectors. There's been a major uptick of interest in Nick Stone's work since the show opened. I'm alerting collectors about getting in at the current price level—gallery speak for, "before you can't afford it."

I close two sales by the time Patrick fetches us a late lunch. "How are things going with Justin?" he asks, arranging cartons from Hi-Thai on the conference table.

"Adolescence is actually pretty awful. He's old enough to get into some serious trouble, but too young to fully realize the consequences."

"Have you had the talk about drugs yet?"

I grab a pair of chopsticks and dig in. "He's admitted to

using pot, and hinted about wanting to try other drugs. It's those that worry me."

"Being gay and taking drugs pretty much goes together at a certain age, especially the club drugs."

"Like ecstasy, you mean?" I did that once with a lady friend, and fell in love with her for the night. A week later I had a breakdown of sorts, identity temporarily scrambled.

"It's mostly crystal meth these days," says Patrick. "It makes for the most amazing sex."

"You aren't using it, are you?" I envision all my mentoring going up in smoke.

"Daniel would drop me in an instant if I did."

"You have a great future. I'm sure you won't fuck it up."

My cell rings. "Justin never showed at the restaurant," says Karen. "We called him, but he didn't pick up. Did his plans change?"

I pretend not to be alarmed. "He must have decided to do something else at the last minute and forgot to tell me. I'm sorry about the mix-up. Thank you both again for volunteering. I'll make it up to you."

I attempt to reach Justin, and keep calling while distracting myself by contacting collectors. Just before closing time, my phone rings.

"Is this Robert Burton?" The woman's voice sounds ominously official. "This is Sarah Wheeler, admissions assistant at Zuckerberg SF General. Justin Woods was admitted to emergency services thirty-five minutes ago. You were listed as a local emergency contact on his phone."

The red-haired receptionist takes my name and asks me to have a seat. I search for an admissions clerk to get more information.

She assures me that someone from the medical staff will be out to talk with me soon. I give her my phone number along with Kat's and Brian's numbers.

A thousand scenarios tumble through my head: Justin hit by a car, accosted by someone on the street, struck by falling debris at a construction site.

I take a seat in the waiting room. A Latino man limps in, bleeding through his pants and shouting for help. Paramedics maneuver a gurney with a sheet-covered figure through the open glass doors.

The first time I came to County General Hospital as it was then called, I had torn the palm of my right hand on a rusty gate. It required ten stitches. Not so long after, I returned far too many times to sit with dozens of friends in the AIDS ward.

A young man, his tie loosened and sleeves rolled-up, approaches and sits on the edge of a chair next to me.

"Mr. Burton, I'm Doctor Fennerman. Since you're not Justin's legal guardian, I can only tell you that we received a 911 call reporting that your nephew was acting erratically, running in and out of traffic on Duboce Street."

"Jesus Christ! How is he? Can I see him?"

"I'm afraid that it will be a while. I can tell you that his condition is stable. We ran a few tests, and we're trying to get him to talk." He places his hand gently on my shoulder, which does little to reassure me, before he excuses himself.

I forgot to ask him if anyone here has called Kat and Brian yet. I take a few deep breaths before I dial. "I'm at the hospital, Kat. It's Justin. He's in the ER."

"Oh my God." My sister's voice rises an octave. "What happened? Is he okay?"

"They haven't told me much, except that he was on the street acting strangely."

"I have a call coming in," she croaks. "It's the hospital. I'll call you back."

I let Patrick know that I won't be returning to the gallery.

"I figured," he says. "How's Justin?"

"I don't really know anything yet."

Dr. Fennerman appears again. "I've just spoken with Justin's parents. They gave permission to fill you in. Your nephew arrived in the ER sweating profusely and breathing rapidly. His pupils were dilated. He said that he had used crystal meth. Judging from his condition, we believe that it may have been cut with something. There's a methamphetamine epidemic on the streets. People are dying from these new combinations, but Justin is young and healthy. His heart valves are resilient and he should pull out of this okay. You can see him now."

I follow a nurse to the room. Someone behind closed curtains coughs spastically. Justin lies in the hospital bed with an IV line attached to his arm. He's slack-jawed, with his mouth agape. He's as pale as the sheet that covers him.

"He's been sedated," the nurse informs. "But you can sit with him if you'd like."

I gaze at the boy, my nephew, and listen to his heavy breathing. It's heartbreaking to see him so messed up like this. And maddening that he did this to himself.

I push aside his frosted forelock to caress his forehead. I'm surprised by how old my hand appears against his skin. I think of all my friends who have died here.

Back in the waiting room, I call Kat.

"I've left two messages for you," she complains, her voice grabbing me by the sleeve. "Brian's absolutely frantic. The doctor said that Justin used methamphetamine." From her stifled sobs, I can tell that she's trying to keep it together. "They said they need to keep him under observation for at least the night. I'm trying to get a flight out this evening."

"There's nothing you can do here. Why don't you wait?"

"I'm his mother! I should be with him."

"I promise to keep you posted. If Justin is well enough to return home in a couple days, I'll fly back with him."

"We never should have sent him out there. It was expecting too much. How could you let this happen, Robert?"

"I'm not his shepherd, Kat."

"You're still thoughtless and irresponsible."

"What do you mean by that?" I try to understand her sudden explosion. I realize that she's upset, but her accusation comes totally out of the blue.

"When you left home, you left me alone to deal with all the repercussions. Mom and Dad's hysteria. Being humiliated every Sunday while the congregation prayed for my sinful brother's return. Classmates treating me like poison because my brother was queer."

"Why are you bringing this up now, Kat?"

"I might have kept my baby if I'd had my brother at home to defend me."

Her words bite deep, deeper than I can handle at the moment. "Please don't do this. You have Justin to think about."

"We shouldn't have put you in this position. That's all I'm saying." She hangs up.

But she's saying so much more. Kat and I were raised in an environment riddled with guilt, saturated in shame. I left that upbringing, but I know it still clings to me, like dirt on a gardener's hands. I never once regretted my decision to leave, and it never occurred to me that my sudden departure was so traumatic for my sister. She must have felt very alone. I buckle inside as a rush of regret overtakes me.

My back is aching. I glance around the waiting room and spot a nice big overstuffed chair designed for some patient's grandmother. Exhausted, I lay my head against the backrest.

My friend Adam raises his bony arm to draw me closer, and whispers, "You need to survive so that you can bury us." I protest that he isn't going to die, that he'll beat the virus.

But I know better, and he does too. He grabs me with his gnarled hand and shakes me, croaking: "I know what's in store for me. Don't pretend you don't...

A nurse stands over me, jiggling my shoulder. "Mr. Burton, your nephew is awake. He's asking for you."

I follow her through a dozen hallways to the main hospital where Justin's been moved. An IV line is still attached to his arm, but I'm relieved to see that color has returned to his face.

He stares up at me and speaks in a weak voice. "I guess I screwed up."

"It looks like you did." I don't want to push things, but I'm not going to pretend either. I think of Adam's words from my dream.

"They said I was dodging cars, but I don't remember."

"You were apparently acting like a drunken bullfighter. You could have been killed."

"Do Mom and Dad know?"

"Your mother wants to fly out here."

"Please, don't let her take me back to Baltimore," he pleads. "Can't I stay with you?"

"You're still a minor, Justin. Your parents make the decisions."

He tries to sit up, wincing "My summer will be totally fucked. I know they'll send me to rehab."

"I'm afraid that you may have sent yourself."

He shrugs, clearly disappointed. "Whatever."

"*Whatever* were you thinking?"

"I don't want to talk about it," he moans, and turns away.

Bridling at his adolescent response, I head for the door. "I'll leave you alone then. I'll see you in the morning."

At the airport, Justin and I hug, until he pulls away and stares me in the eye.

"I met this guy," he confesses. "He took me to his apartment and gave me something so that we could have more fun. And then he kicked me out."

I could be the instructive uncle, but instead, I tell him, "You're going to be okay. I'm sure you'll never take that risk again."

The strained expression he's carried since he was released from the hospital seems to lift, and he shakes my hand. "I hope I wasn't a big disappointment."

"You're going to be okay," I tell him. He takes a place in line and moves to the TSA checkpoint. He flips off his shoes, hoists his backpack onto the luggage belt, and recovers his belongings on the other side before pulling his hoodie over his head. Then, suddenly intent on his phone's bright screen, he disappears into the crowd of summer travelers.

My heart lurches. I feel astonishingly empty now that he's gone.

I reach Kat. "Justin's at the gate now. His flight is scheduled to arrive in Baltimore on time." I don't reveal what Justin has just confided.

She lets out a sigh. "I'm sorry about what I said to you, Robert. It was just too terrible to think that I might lose Justin. Thank you for taking him on. I know it wasn't easy."

My sister has calmed down, but the pain is still there. We have some tough things to talk through, circumstances we've ignored for a very long time.

"I want you to know," she says, "Brian and I are sending Justin to rehab for the rest of the summer."

I wince, imagining how he will receive the news. Still, I tell her that it's the right thing to do.

At home, Tigre emerges from under his hiding place at last and purrs at my feet. Neither of us were accustomed to the disarray Justin brought to our lives. This makes me miss him, though only for a moment, before I fall into bed exhausted.

I wake up hours later and throw cold water on my face, noticing creases that I've never seen before. It's the result of keeping close watch over someone so young for several days, I suppose. I shuffle into the kitchen and open the top cabinet where I stashed the liquor before Justin arrived.

I pour myself a drink and stare out at the city through a rare summer drizzle. Red and white lights are snaking in opposite directions on the freeway. The LED display at the top of the Salesforce Tower emits abstract images of what appears to be a modern dance performance replicating strobe-light syndrome. Sirens pulse and wail from different parts of the city, like a percussive symphony.

I'm relieved now that Justin has left. But also sadder than when he first arrived, and when everything seemed possible between us.

About the Author

William Torphy's short stories have been featured in podcasts and have appeared in numerous magazines and journals, including *Bryant Literary Review, The Fictional Café, Sun Star Quarterly, Chelsea Station, Arlington Literary Journal,* and *Adelaide Literary Magazine.* His opinion pieces and reviews have been featured in *Solstice Literary, OpEdge, Vox Populi* and *The Dalhousie Review.* Ithuriel's Spear Press has published "Love Never Always," a poetry collection; "Snakebite," young adult fiction; and "A Brush With History," a biography of California activist and artist Eda Kavin. He has recently moved to Wisconsin from the San Francisco Bay area where he served the arts community as an exhibition curator. www.williamtorphy.com

About Unsolicited Press

Unsolicited Press is based out of Portland, Oregon and focuses on the works of the unsung and underrepresented. As a womxn-owned, all-volunteer small publisher that doesn't worry about profits as much as championing exceptional literature, we have the privilege of partnering with authors skirting the fringes of the lit world. We've worked with emerging and award-winning authors such as Shann Ray, Amy Shimshon-Santo, Brook Bhagat, Kris Amos, and John W. Bateman.

Learn more at unsolicitedpress.com. Find us on twitter and instagram.

www.ingramcontent.com/pod-product-compliance
Lightning Source LLC
Chambersburg PA
CBHW050844190726
48286CB00007B/2225